SISTER SPIRIT

'A supernatural thriller about family, ancestry
and belonging.'

The Bookseller, One to Watch

'You are in for an absolute treat! A Nigerian boarding
school adventure, featuring myth, magic, friendship,
romance, plus Yoruba magic and history. Truly
original and mesmerising YA.'

Lindsay Galvin, author of *Call of the Titanic*

'*Sister Spirit* kept me turning the pages. A story about
identity, culture and African myth. Set against the
backdrop of a Nigerian boarding school, *Sister Spirit* is
creepy, haunting, yet filled with history, loss, hope and
love. Efua has once again written a brilliant book with
the best Nigerian representation.'

Abiola Bello, author of
The Very Merry Murder Club

'Efua Traoré's gripping and atmospheric YA debut hits so many sweet spots: convincing historical fiction blended with a gothic mystery, boarding school drama, and a budding romance.'

Ayesha Harruna Attah, author of
The Deep Blue Between

'*Sister Spirit* is an intense and addictive supernatural thriller, blending a powerful mystery with a gripping emotional journey of self-discovery and identity. Efua's writing is an immersive and captivating experience, drawing the reader into this unique and powerful world.'

J.P. Rose, author of
The Haunting of Tyrese Walker

'A poignant story of family and identity told in Efua Traoré's incredibly unique voice. Efua writes in a way that is both lyrical but also grounded and I was deftly transported into Tara's story, and hooked as she explored the complexities of her past and her identity. A stunning book!'

Alwyn Hamilton, author of *Rebel of the Sands*

SISTER
SPIRIT

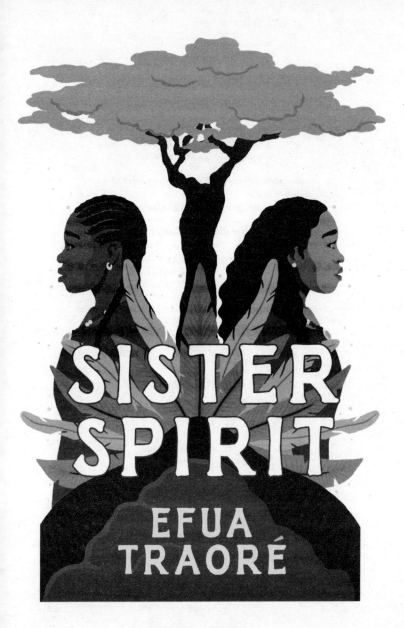

SISTER SPIRIT

EFUA TRAORÉ

ZEPHYR

An imprint of Head of Zeus

Cover illustration: Camilla Ru
Typesetting: Ed Pickford

Printed and bound in Great Britain by
CPI Group (UK) Ltd, Croydon CR0 4YY

Head of Zeus Ltd
First Floor East
5–8 Hardwick Street
London EC1R 4RG

WWW.HEADOFZEUS.COM

To all those searching…

…may you find home.

ENGLAND

PROLOGUE

A sharp gust of wind tore at her shawl, unleashing long dark curls. She slipped in her haste to get out of the window, scraping her thigh. A bruise bloomed on her pale skin, visible even in the feeble moonlight.

Ignoring the throb, she hauled her other leg off the ledge, ripping her thin nightgown.

Gathering the ruined dress at the skirts, she stumbled into the night. The urge was so strong she could hardly bear it. Her breath came in gasps, not from exhaustion, but from a need to be quicker. She padded swiftly across the lawn, through soft moss between trees and over sharp and wicked undergrowth, not slowing, until she felt the cold hardness of rock.

She could hear it. The roar ahead.

She was almost there.

Clouds shifted, and the moon lit a vast expanse of ocean. Cliffs jutted harshly out of the landscape. The force of the wind tore at her from all sides.

Feeling the urge more strongly than ever, she lunged forward, toes curling around the edge of the cliff. And with a searing pain in her chest, she stretched out her arms, and let loose a long, heart-wrenching wail.

'Jiiimiii...!'

1

I glared at the poster stuck to the classroom door. It was faded, its edges discoloured, begging to be ripped off. I imagined tearing it down, strip after strip, skinning the door, until there was nothing left.

Chase your dreams.

I scoffed silently at the worn-out words.

What if your dreams were chasing you? But you had to step into them, night after night. No matter how badly it hurt to do so.

'Tara Walther!'

I was jerked out of my thoughts by an angry voice.

'Would you kindly give us a moment of your attention?' Mrs Jacobs was standing in front of my desk, peering at me with eyebrows that grated together.

'Sorry, Mrs Jacobs,' I mumbled, shielding my notebook. The entire page was covered with sketches of the young woman on the cliff. The dream had long since taken over my nights. It now threatened to take over my days. I closed my notebook with a sigh, trying to get the images out of my head.

Someone sniggered and I looked up to find Mrs Jacobs still staring at me. 'We were at genealogy and family history. The history of your surname. Did you get that?'

'Oh, ehm … yes, Walther is an old Germanic name, as far as I know.'

A collective giggle rose up. Hot blood rushed to my face, flushing my cheeks. I knew I didn't look Germanic with my curly afro and brown skin. In fact, there was no resemblance between me and my parents. But that was not surprising, since I was adopted.

Mrs Jacobs let out a gasp of exasperation. 'I wasn't asking for an answer now, I want a one-page essay and a family tree of four generations next week. It is the class homework.'

'Oh!' I lowered my head, realising my mistake.

Recently, I'd become so sensitive about 'being different'. I knew why. It was the dream. The more I dreamed of her, the more I wanted to know who she was. Could the woman possibly be my—

The metallic ring of the bell sounded. Chairs pushed back abruptly and everyone began grabbing their books.

Maxine caught my eye. She was heading over with a rueful half-smile. I knew I could count on her not to

4

have sniggered. She would not say anything about what had happened, and we would have lunch and talk about everything and nothing. About TikToks, the next book on our shared TBR pile or season four of our favourite anime. Anything but our feelings. Then we'd walk home together, as we'd lived on the same street since we were little. That's how it had always been.

I didn't know how else to be. How do you talk about your feelings when you don't even know yourself?

Before Maxine reached my desk, I snatched up my notebook and my school bag and ran.

2

I tried slipping noiselessly into the house, but Mum called out, 'Hello, hon! Back so early?'

'Yeah! There was nothing good for lunch and I wasn't hungry,' I lied.

'I don't have anything ready yet.'

'I'm not hungry!' I called back, flinging my rucksack in the corner.

Previous generations of Walthers in stiff white collars stared down at me from the photos on the wall. I thought of our annoying family-tree homework and cringed.

I was definitely not submitting that one.

Agnes and Ludwig Walther looked disapproving so I glanced at Grandma Lisbeth and Grandpa Matheus, who I preferred anyway. I had memories of their cosy place surrounded by green hills, the scent of fresh scones wafting through a tiny kitchen with red-and-white checked curtains. Grandma's arms holding me while she read aloud in her quiet voice. Dad and Grandpa taking me fishing. Had I felt more at ease as a child? Had I worried less about who I was? These wisps of memories felt so carefree.

I glanced at the photo of me sitting on Dad's lap and Mum leaning in with a smile. They looked ... proud. I must have been about four. I studied my face, trying to see past the sharp contrast of my brownness and full black hair and my pale, blond parents. I was smiling in the photo. So there must have been a time when I felt happier. But since the dreams began, my memories had become muddled. Most of the time, I felt numb.

'Should I cook up some pesto noodles?' Mum called.

'Goodness, Margie, she said she's not hungry! Could you please stop shouting across the house, I'm trying to work!' Dad's voice close by made me jump.

He was sitting at the dining table, his long, thin frame hunched over a mass of papers that spilled around him. Dad was an architect and often worked from home, turning the living room into a mess of construction plans, laptop and pencils.

Dad's greying hair half-covered his thick glasses, much too long in Mum's opinion.

'Hey, Tara, everything okay?' he asked, looking over his glasses and stretching out an arm. Normally we weren't hugging types but maybe he sensed something.

A craving for the safe comfort seeping out of the photos overcame me and without replying I walked over and folded myself into his embrace.

I sat up in bed gasping for air. This time the dream had felt so real.

Taking deep, ragged breaths, the wet, cold cotton of my pyjamas peeled off like a disgusting second skin.

My insides felt like a tight fist. The shadows in my room still resembled grey rock jutting like knives around me.

Suddenly the floor gave way and a gust of wind rushed in. The familiar roar of waves smashing against the cliffs tore through the air and an abyss loomed in front of me. I screamed and grasped the sides of my bed. But instead of soft mattress, my fingers scratched hard rock.

And there she was, a few steps ahead, arms outstretched to the darkness beyond.

Then a bright light and a rush of warm dusty air blinded me and the scenery rushed past like a fast-moving train. I held on to the sharp protruding rock, my insides jerking, as dark woods became lush green jungle and dank earth turned to red sand.

Everything went still. The rock beneath my sweaty palms felt warmer, smoother, more rounded. The grey ocean was gone. A strange tree stood tall, its roots tucked into hard stone at its base. The woman had disappeared, along with the grey cliffs, fading in the sunlight.

Sadness filled me, weighing me down. My limbs trembled and I tried to get a better hold, but my fingers slipped and I began to fall into nothingness.

I screamed and I was back in my bedroom, back on my pillow with my sweat-soaked neck, and Dad and Mum bent over me, with worried, sleep-drunken faces.

3

'**M**axine brought your school work.'

I lay sprawled across my bed, trying to concentrate on a book.

Mum stood uncertainly in the doorway and Lulu slunk in between her legs. She purred at me, a fluffy red monster and I stroked her cloud-like fur.

Mum dropped the papers on my desk. 'She said to tell you get well soon and that your homework is page sixty-five for maths and to read the article and answer the questions for English.'

'Okay, thanks.'

Maxine had obviously not asked to come in. I sighed. What was I doing? Ignoring her messages, avoiding her in school, rejecting her efforts to keep up our friendship. I guessed she was finally giving up on me.

The doctor had also given up. Said there was nothing wrong, at least nothing physical. *It's psychological*, she'd said.

Now, after one week at home since the last dream, the pain in my chest had eased and my breathing was normal. But the burning throb in my veins was there. The empty feeling in my insides, the yearning.

'Well, I'll leave you to your homework,' Mum said quietly. 'Is there anything I can do for you? Bring you something? A Coke?' Her eyes were searching, anxious.

I shook my head and she closed the door.

I flung my book aside. Why couldn't I be less complicated? Not have them worrying about me all the time. Sometimes I thought: *Did they regret choosing me?*

I grabbed my phone and began typing:

Thanks for bringing the homework, Max! Sorry for not replying. I know I'm not the friend I should be right now. I just need to sort myself out. Please forgive me.

I deleted the 'Please forgive me' part and pressed *Send*. Maybe the school work would help take my mind off things.

The sun had gone past my window, casting long shadows across the wooden floor. I switched on my lamp and sat down, rubbing my temples. My limbs turned heavy at the thought of night, the thought of the dream.

She wanted to tell me something, I could sense it. I had so many questions. *Who was Jimi or Jimmy? Why did she call him, with so much grief? Was he a son? A lost love?*

What scared me most was that it did not feel like a dream. It felt like a memory.

I had never been interested in my biological parents. Mum and Dad had asked twice before if I wanted to talk about the adoption. The first time was when I was five. I had come home from school crying. 'Why do I look different? I don't want to be brown. I want to be like you.' I still cringed at the memory. They'd stared in horror, not knowing what to say. When they'd finally found their voice and started telling me of another mummy, it made things worse. 'I don't want another mummy,' I had screamed. It was bad enough being different from everyone else around me. But having another mummy or daddy was even more scary.

The next time was when I was ten years old. Some silly kid made a comment at a school summer picnic. 'Look at that funny family! That girl doesn't look like her parents. Why is she so dark and they're so white?' The kid's mum had been embarrassed and shushed him. I would have loved to forget the whole thing, but that evening Mum and Dad asked if I wanted to talk. What they didn't know was that I often heard such comments. It was nothing new. I had learned to ignore them.

But now things had changed. I had questions. Lots of them.

I had to know if the woman in my dreams was a memory. If she was my mother.

⌐⌐⌐

'How old was I?'

Mum and Dad were cleaning the kitchen after dinner. My question came out as a half-croaked sentence, but I could see by their quick glances they knew what I meant.

Mum cleared her throat. 'You mean, when we—'

'Yes!' I cut her short. 'How old was I when you adopted me?' I couldn't look at them and slipped into a chair at the kitchen table.

Mum wiped her hands on her jeans.

'Are you sure this is a good time?' Mum began.

Dad raised an eyebrow, but Mum carried on. 'Honey, does this have something to do with your nightmares? Is that what they're about?'

I felt a twinge of guilt and shook my head. 'I want to know about myself. I am ready now.'

'Oh, Tara, of course!' Mum said, fiercely whipping her ponytail.

Dad didn't beat around the bush. 'You were two years old,' he said. He was doing his best to sound matter of fact, but I could see from his stiff shoulders that he was as nervous as Mum and I.

By delaying this conversation, I had allowed the crack between us to become a huge valley. And now I stood far away on the other side, trying to find a bridge back to them. Or was it a bridge back to myself?

'I was only two?'

'Is that a bad thing?' Mum asked. 'It was lovely to have you so young. We thought we could bond better.'

'I have these memories sometimes and I kind of thought...'

'They were from your previous family?' Dad asked.

I nodded, fighting back tears.

'Those memories,' Mum began, 'are they the nightmares?'

I nodded again and tried to ignore the worry in her eyes.

'It's not likely, though,' Dad said. 'Two is young.'

'I know,' I said, biting my lip.

'We don't know anything about your biological parents, Tara.' Mum spoke carefully, as if trying not to wake a sleeping beast. 'There was only your biological mother, unfortunately...' She glanced at Dad.

'She's dead, right?' I asked.

It was strange, but I knew. They nodded. 'I'm so sorry,' Mum said.

'We have something of hers,' Dad said, with a quick uncertain glance at Mum. 'Do you want to see it?'

It was a slim silvery-blue book, worn around the edges. A diary without dates, just irregular spaces between entries. And they were not really sentences. More like words strung together without meaning. Bizarre sketches that didn't make sense, squeezed in at odd angles.

The more pages I turned, the more worried I became. There were skulls and bloody images. My breath caught at a hand holding a human head, fingers clawed into intricately woven hair, face contorted, blood dripping from a severed throat. I slammed the book shut.

My dreams could not possibly be memories because I had been too young. Now the only person who could have supplied answers was dead, her diary a grotesque mess.

Dad had warned me. After placing the book in my hand he'd drawn me into an awkward hug. 'Her notes might be difficult. We went through them looking for information.' He seemed embarrassed. 'We needed to know if there was anything about what you liked to eat or if you had allergies. There was nothing. I … I think she wasn't well.'

An ice-cold thought crystallised in my mind. What if I was going crazy too?

I skimmed more pages, then threw the book on to my desk. But before the book closed, I saw something that made me freeze. Something familiar. A word scribbled beneath a drawing of a rock, massive and rounded with a large tree.

I grabbed the book and flipped through it with trembling fingers.

I knew it.

I was right.

A rock I recognised. And the word... I stared at it, almost choking. Written in shaky letters and blotched, as if a tear had dropped and dissolved the ink:

... Ji ... mi ...

4

'**D**ad, this is so important to me,' I cried, gripping the backrest of the sofa and kneading the cushion.

I couldn't explain what was happening, but since that new dream of the rock with the tree, my life had only one goal: to go there. I had spent nights scrolling articles and pages about rocks around the world, rocks surrounded by distant jungles. Finally one night, when my eyes were a tired, burning mess, one sharp image had stood out and all my alarms had begun ringing at once. A sacred rock called Olumo in a city called Abeokuta in Nigeria. The tree rooted in it was called an Iroko tree. I had a feeling of absolute certainty that I would find out everything about myself there.

In Nigeria!

'Well, we could contact the adoption agency or social services,' Dad said slowly. 'Then find out if there is a link to Nigeria. We don't know what nationality your biological parents had.'

'Maybe they can give us the contact details of your biological father,' Mum said gently. 'He would be the best person to give you the answers you need.'

I shook my head impatiently. I couldn't explain. It was more than just knowing. It was an urge, burning me on the inside, calling me.

'I understand this is important to you, but we can't jump up and fly to a country we don't know. To visit a rock in your dream!' Dad was pacing the room now.

I tried to speak calmly. 'I do not need confirmation from any council or agency. I know this sounds crazy, but I am absolutely sure about this.'

Mum winced at the word crazy and Dad joined her on the sofa. The fear was in their eyes again. I tried to push away the thought which came every time I was being difficult. *Did they regret adopting me?*

I took a deep breath. 'I had a really clear vision of this rock with the tree,' I began. Mum buried her face in her hands.

'Tara, things have been hard on you these past weeks. I think we should consider you going back to therapy.'

I shook my head and jumped up. 'I am not crazy!'

'No one thinks you are,' Dad said. 'We feel you need someone to talk to. Someone who understands these things.'

'I am not going back to Dr Shuklah. This has nothing to do with my mental health. I feel perfectly fine.' I charged out and ran to my room, slamming the door.

The lamp on my desk cast a bright circle of light. The silvery-blue diary was lying just outside it, in the shadows. Like all the things I badly needed to understand, it seemed to want to stay in the dark, out of reach.

I spent the next few days in bed and refused to go back to school.

We didn't speak about the matter again until they called me into the living room.

'We contacted the agency and social services,' Dad said, pushing strands of hair behind his ears.

I nibbled at my fingernail. 'And?'

'They didn't have much information. Your biological mother had been estranged from her family. Her name was Ruth Bensworth.'

I swallowed. Ruth. It was strange hearing a name that should have meant something to me.

'Bensworth was her maiden name. She wasn't married and lived alone in a small flat,' Dad went on. 'According to a recorded statement from a concerned elderly neighbour, she didn't have friends or family come to see her. She was very reserved.'

Dad took a deep breath before continuing. 'There were attempts…' he said. 'Attempts to contact her family after she passed. All efforts failed. There was a grandfather, but he refused to be involved. The council received strict orders to leave him out of anything to do with Ruth. They couldn't give us his name or contact details.'

There was an odd silence. I felt their eyes on me.

My insides dropped. Not because no one had wanted me, although that stung a bit, but because if she lived as a recluse, then my hopes of finding out more were dashed. I didn't see any way of convincing my parents to take me to Olumo Rock.

'Was that all?' I asked.

Dad shifted in his seat. Mum stared at her fingers entwined in her lap.

'Dad, Mum, please! I need to find out what this is all about. Why the rock was so important to her and why she killed herself.'

'What did you say?' Mum's voice was almost a shriek.

'We never told you that. How do you know?' Dad asked. 'Did she write anything in that diary? I shouldn't have given it to you. We've made matters worse.'

'No, she didn't write anything about that,' I said quickly. 'Most of her words don't make sense. She was obviously a troubled person. I think she had the same strong urge I feel. A yearning. I don't know why, but I feel the same way.'

Dad and Mum darted quick glances at each other.

'Why would you assume she killed herself?' Mum asked.

'I … I just know she ended her own life,' I said. 'I can't explain it.'

They stared at me without speaking. Fear flitted like dark shadows across their eyes. Mum loosened Dad's tight fist and slipped her hand in his.

'Well,' Dad sighed. 'The social services confirmed what the neighbour said. That your biological father had never been in the picture, but seeing that you were brown and looked different from Ruth, she had once asked Ruth about him. Ruth mentioned he was from Nigeria.'

I jumped up.

'Do you believe me now?'

Dad raised his hands. 'This doesn't mean anything. It could be a coincidence.'

'What?' I interrupted him. 'You can't possibly think that.'

'Mum?'

Mum shrugged. Her grey eyes looked tired and her jaw tight with worry. 'We really think things have gone too far. This is not good for you. Have you considered trying to put this behind you? It's making you ill.'

'It's *not* knowing that's making me ill, Mum. Weird dreams, shreds of memories I can't put together.'

I stomped out, heading for my room and my laptop.

I opened the search engine and began typing words: *Bensworth, property, coastal, cliffs, England.*

5

This was one of my worst ideas. I stared through the gates at the large house, overgrown with ivy. Gnarled trees clawed at the roof with withered branches, casting it in shadow. It might once have been a cheerful pale yellow, but now it was a faded grey, with a mossy roof, cracked walls and tall, looming windows. I had travelled three hundred kilometres from home, lying to Mum and Dad, and the school. Now I was here, disappointment weighed on me. I didn't recognise it.

I turned to the gate: cold and rough with rust and age, but the harshness against my palms steadied me. I felt a strange sensation, like I was being watched. I glanced at the house and noticed movement in a window. A face caught my eye, then was gone.

I rang the bell.

A minute later I rang it again. And again. It must have been five minutes before the front door creaked open.

An old man walked slowly towards me. He looked like he had dressed for a ball at the beginning of the previous century, but decided to keep the clothes on for the rest of his life. They were ancient and sagging, and yet from the way he carried himself with his hair perfectly combed, he wore them with pride.

Dull eyes, a diluted grey that, like the house, might have been some other brighter colour in the past, took in every angle of my face. For a split-second, I thought there was a hardening in his features, but he did not speak.

'My name is Tara Walther,' I ventured, my voice not quite as steady as I'd hoped. 'I am the daughter of Ruth Bensworth.'

The deep lines around his thin lips and eyes remained rigid like a mask and I wasn't sure if he'd understood me. He leaned back, as if wanting to turn away, and my breath snagged at the thought of him leaving me there. Then he reached for the lock and the gates screeched as the rust was pried apart.

I followed him in a daze, through tall, creaky doors and a musty hall, covered with emblems, family crests, pith helmets, paintings and antlers. A glass cabinet displayed chunky beige bracelets intricately decorated, that looked very much like ivory. The man walked slowly, his head high despite his thin, bent back.

We arrived in a gloomy room and I had a strange impulse to giggle. The study, like the rest of the house, was a stubborn relic of the past. The windows were blocked by thick, blood-red curtains and the room was heavy with a stale smell of mould. An old leather sofa was lit by a dim, emerald-green lamp. I felt like darting to the window and tearing it open. The old man had sat in the darkest corner, watching me with sharp eyes.

I took a step towards him.

'That's close enough,' he said in a thin voice. 'What do you want?'

My cheeks flushed. I hadn't expected much from a person who abandoned his own motherless granddaughter, but if this was my grandfather I was stunned by his coldness.

'I am looking for information about my birth mother,' I said.

A clock ticked somewhere. It sounded encumbered, as if even time had grown old and slowed in this place.

'She left long ago.'

'I need to know … things … I don't know anything about my biological father or my … about Ruth's past. I need to understand…' I stopped. How could I say what I wanted? I couldn't tell him my dreams had brought me here.

The old man leaned forward. His body came out of the shadows and his face was hard in the dull light.

'It hasn't stopped, has it? As her daughter, a female Bensworth, you carry the curse. That is why you are here, is it not so?'

'A c-curse?' I stammered. 'What curse?'

'For generations, the women in this family have brought only grief, shame and horror. When will it end?'

I stumbled back. Fears swarmed my head like ravens crowding a tree, filling every nook.

His scrawny hands clawed at his throat. Trembling fingers loosened the silk tie at his collar. He coughed weakly.

'I knew it was best to keep away from her child. As soon as I heard it was a girl.'

'I do not understand, what curse? What do you mean?'

His eyes focused on mine. 'For over one hundred and fifty years, every female Bensworth has lived a cursed life. All were plagued by nightly visions, an ill mind and a pain of the heart that could not be healed. Each one died at a young age. Each one died at their own hand.'

I shook my head so violently my vision blurred.

'You may leave now.'

I tried to focus my jumbled mind. This couldn't be all. He had to have something for me. A clue as to what the dreams were about. This was not a curse. It was a puzzle that needed solving. It had to do with that rock.

'But there must have been a reason?' I persisted. 'If I could just understand what it was...'

He sat back in his chair. 'It is the curse,' he mumbled and closed his eyes. 'It is the curse.'

As I tripped down the path towards the gates, I heard it. The distant sound of waves crashing.

Then I was running back and around the house. I caught sight of him, watching me from the window, but I didn't care.

I ran through neglected bushes and flowerbeds between the trees. I recognised the window she had climbed out of and traced my fingers across the ledge while I caught my breath. I continued down the path where I had followed her, so many times before.

Across the lawn, now a rough stretch of weeds and wild flowers, and through soft moss under mushroom-sprouting trees. The air became thick with fog and my foot caught twice in roots. She'd run here barefoot at night. I did not slow until I felt the hardness of rock beneath my trainers and the spray of salt air in my nostrils. A large expanse of sky opened above me.

There it was. The raging ocean and the curved outline of ragged cliffs. Exactly like in my dream.

The urge in my chest hit me, stronger than ever. I stretched out my arms towards the ocean, took a deep gulp of air, and let out a long, liberating cry.

NIGERIA

6

The moment we landed in Lagos my breathing steadied, as if a knot had loosened and my organs twisted free. My head felt like a crown of feathers.

Dusty, reddish browns and greens spread beyond the runway and the city stood vibrant in the distance.

I drank the spicy, earthy air in greedy gulps. I couldn't get enough of it.

'Goodness,' Dad gasped. 'This has to be the hottest, heaviest air I have ever breathed.' His forehead looked like a film of bubble wrap, beads of sweat sprouting and forming in rows.

I grinned and patted his shoulder, still not quite believing they'd allowed me to come. After our huge row about me ditching school and going off on the train to look for my biological grandfather, I'd thought it was over. But when they'd calmed down and realised the lengths I was willing to go to, they'd softened.

They'd decided Dad would take me on a short visit during summer holidays. I had agreed to all conditions, of course: going back to Dr Shuklah, improving my grades and making more effort with Maxine and my social life. Anything.

Despite our six-hour flight, I hadn't wanted to spend the night in Lagos, and urged Dad that we go straight to Abeokuta, the city of the rock. A taxi drove us to the bus stop, then it was just under two more hours on the road.

The wait for the bus was a loud, cinematic experience. There were crowds of shouting, sweaty people, music blasting from loudspeakers and taxis and buses exploding with luggage, passengers and animals. Screeching chickens in wicker baskets and bleating goats were stacked on lorries. Dad gripped my arm so tight it hurt, but I didn't care. I was too excited. He paid a young bare-chested man with sharp muscles to get us on a bus. The man took Dad's bag and threw it on his shoulder, beckoning us to follow. I stumbled after, my heavy rucksack swaying left and right.

'Commot for road jareh, make una move,' he shouted, urging people out of the way, as if we were VIPs.

A huge tray swooped down like a UFO. I shrieked, dodging it, and caught sight of fresh coconut slices and bright yellow pineapple chunks balanced on a woman's head. She swerved and steadied the wobbling tray with one hand. Cool water splashed enticingly on my face, but Dad was pulling me forward.

'Oyinbo wan enter bus to Abeokuta,' the young man called to a guy with a shiny bald head, who was stuffing boxes into the boot of a rickety mini-van. The van was bursting with passengers, who all turned to stare at Dad.

'Oyinbo, sorry oh, plenty heat today,' a young woman with a tray of water bottles on her head called to Dad.

The people in the bus sniggered and watched Dad curiously as he fanned himself with his passport.

'You wan buy cold wota?' the woman asked.

Dad shook his head, looking flustered and I squeezed his hand.

The young man handed Dad's bag to the driver. 'Oga tank you, bye-bye,' he said, disappearing into the crowd.

The driver indicated for us to enter.

'Oya, oya, make una move,' he shouted at the passengers inside.

I heaved my rucksack off and squeezed into the back row beside three women. They were wearing clothes sewn in the same dark red-and-purple fabric. Their head ties, made from thick glittery orange material, brushed the roof of the bus. Dad tucked into the middle row of seats between two men, still looking overwhelmed. The driver turned the radio on full volume and we were off!

I couldn't stop grinning at the thought of Dad's face. I didn't mind the heat or the noise. The afro-beat music and the radio moderator with his Nigerian-English accent were a pure dose of Nigerian culture. The whole journey felt like an adventure. The women beside me began speaking pidgin English. It had a cool singsong vibe, as if a bland soup of English words had been pimped up with hot and foreign spice. Every now and then I recognised a word and had to stop myself from trying to say it out loud.

The van wobbled through roads with huge potholes and a traffic jam with people dodging between cars selling things through open windows. The sidewalks bustled with colourful contrasts – monotone grey suits, floor-length white kaftans with intricate golden embroideries, mid-length kaftans worn with trousers, beautiful dresses in bright African cloth, as well as regular jeans and shorts with T-shirts. The head gear was amazing too – some men wore little caps while the women wore hijabs or tall head ties like oversized crowns. Other women had delicately woven hair piled up in a bun or falling down to the waist in braided waves.

With the melodic soundtrack of the women beside me, I leaned back into the seat. A shiver of excitement rolled over me. Finally, I was here.

7

My breath came deep and calm as I stood facing the horizon, the world at my feet. I was really here, on the rock of my dreams! A warm wind caressed my cheek and my eyes burned with tears.

Dad placed a hand on my shoulder. 'Your rock is beautiful,' he said softly.

I nodded and placed my palms flat against the stone. I knew there were bigger rocks on earth, but there was something magical that I felt in every pore of my body.

Had my biological mother been here? Had she felt safe too? Why had this rock been so important to her? And why was it important to me now?

I took in the panoramic view of the city with its thousands of reddish-brown metal roofs. Olumo Rock was at the centre of everything.

'If you look over there,' our guide, a friendly young woman, said, 'you will see the first church of Nigeria, built by the missionaries in 1844. And there, the River Ogun snaking its way around the city. Do you see that tall building?'

I followed her finger as she pointed out the sights, then something shifted and I blinked. Something weird was happening to the roofs of the buildings. They had lost their harsh coppery, metallic glint and began to look more rounded. Reddish clay huts with thatched roofs spread before me, and there was smoke everywhere! A raging fire was eating up the huts. Gunshots tore through smoke curling into the sky and screams ripped the air.

I jumped back, stumbling.

'Are you okay, Tara?' Dad asked.

I blinked again and my vision cleared. *What was happening to me?*

'The wars must have been awful,' I said shakily, turning to the guide and ignoring Dad's stares. 'Did they survive the attacks?'

The guide looked confused at the change of topic, but nodded. 'There were many wars here, but the Egba people were great warriors.'

I heard the pride in her voice.

'They suffered lots of casualties,' she continued. 'But they were mostly victorious.'

Her voice faded and I felt myself sway.

'Follow me,' she said, 'I will show you the war-time hideouts of the Egba people.'

The guide led us around a large boulder to an opening; one of the many tunnels, caves and crevices inside Olumo Rock.

'The city of Abeokuta was founded in 1830, during the tribal wars, before the first missionaries came,' the guide said. 'Olumo means "the end of our wanderings". The uprooted Egba people found a safe place here. Olumo was a natural fortress where they could hide from their enemies.' She pointed to a smooth entrance and we stooped low to enter.

'Oh, wow, this is amazing,' Dad said.

'This was the kitchen,' the guide said, pointing to rounded holes carved into the ground. 'These were used for grinding and pounding grains or vegetables while in hiding.'

'Who were their enemies?' Dad asked.

'There were prolonged wars between the Egbas and other tribes like the Oyo, Ijebu and Ife people. The Egbas even fought wars against the Dahomians who came all the way from Nigeria's neighbouring country, known as Benin today. The early settlers stayed hidden here and were safe from attack. As more people sought refuge, the city was founded at the foot of the rock and named Abeokuta, which means "town under the rock". By 1850, refugees from all over Yorubaland made Abeokuta one of the largest towns in West Africa.'

'Oh, wow,' Dad said again.

The guide nodded. 'By then Abeokuta was a walled town with fifty thousand people. Some parts of the walls can still be seen today.'

I traced my finger along the stone, which felt strangely familiar.

'The Egba people come regularly for annual festivals,' she was saying.

'Amazing,' Dad said for the twentieth time.

We passed cowrie-studded statues, carvings and the grave of a chief, but I hardly noticed what I was seeing. My legs felt light and I floated after them.

We climbed a narrow passageway and came out before a door built into the rock.

Thick, red streaks were smeared across the wood and I shuddered. The blood had tiny feathers in it, fluttering in the breeze.

'Sacrifices are made to the god of the rock,' the guide was saying. 'People bring animals and the blood is spilled to ask for protection or guidance or wealth. This shrine is opened once a year during the Olumo Festival.'

A gust of wind hissed from beneath the door and a chill crawled across my skin. I stumbled back, my chest tight.

'Tara?' Dad asked.

'I'm fine,' I mumbled. 'I lost my balance.'

But I could feel him scrutinising me.

'Where is the Iroko tree,' I asked quickly.

'Ah, the sacred Iroko tree,' the guide pointed. 'We have to go around that boulder there. Its leaves are only plucked for the coronation of the Alake, the most important chief in Abeokuta. The leaves never wither or fall, even in dry season.'

I hurried towards it, longing to feel something – maybe a vision, like before. The Iroko tree stood, tall and imposing, its long, twisted arms reaching up to the sky. Very gently I placed a hand on the cool, rough trunk.

But I felt nothing – only the breeze stirring. Then, something fluttered off the tree. Had the guide not just said the tree never lost its leaves?

I hurried around grey boulders huddled together, but saw nothing out of place.

As I turned to leave, I noticed a shadow at the side of the path. It was the dark shape of an old woman, draped in a blueish gown that hung loosely off her shoulders.

Feet rooted to the spot, my breath snagged.

She looked frail. The skin on her face and neck were brittle and her eyes were so clouded by cataracts it was like staring into a grey translucent ocean.

'Good afternoon,' I managed, my heart pounding.

Was this the priestess who lived in the rock? The guide had said she was one hundred and thirty years old.

The woman stared at me from the endless pits of her eyes. Had she understood?

A strange feeling came over me, a kind of buzzing that spread from my ears down to my toes. 'You must know the rock like the palm of your hand,' I whispered. 'Do you know why it is calling me?'

Her gaze shifted to something behind me and I heard a shuffling sound.

'This area is out of bounds,' the guide said, coming towards me. 'This is where the priestess lives and out of respect, tourists are not allowed here.'

'Oh, I am sorry,' I mumbled, turning back to apologise. But there was no one there. The old woman had disappeared. As I followed the guide, a headache pulsing at my temple, I heard a low, dry whisper in my ear, like the rustling branches of the Iroko tree.

Those who seek will find ... will find ... will find.

8

'**H**ow are you feeling?' Dad asked over his coffee, toast and jam.

'Great!' I replied, stuffing fried plantains into my mouth. 'These are fantastic, Dad! You should try one. The bean cakes are also delicious, very spicy, but the fried plantains are best.'

Dad smiled nervously at my colourful plate of bean cakes, fried plantains, fried egg and spicy sardine stew.

'I'm fine with this, thanks,' he mumbled into his coffee. 'But you know I didn't mean breakfast, Tara.'

I shrugged. 'Coming here was good ... it was necessary.'

No point trying to explain how being here made me feel. He wouldn't understand. I had no idea why I felt my life depended on it. I only knew that since I'd walked on Nigerian ground, I had been feeling better than ever before.

Dad nodded and looked at me with a strange expression. A flicker of pain crossed his face.

I stretched out my hand to cover his. 'Thanks, Dad, for bringing me here. This is so important to me.'

He looked as if he wanted to say more, but just smiled awkwardly.

I bit my lip. I really wished I could explain things to him.

We ate in silence, each of us lost in thought.

'The pool looks inviting,' Dad said when we'd finished, obviously trying to sound more cheerful and relaxed. 'Join me?'

I looked at the pool glittering beneath palm trees, and shook my head. 'I would love to stroll around the shopping mall down the road.'

Dad frowned. 'I am not too sure about that.'

'I won't be long, Dad. I will be careful! Promise!'

He sighed, then opened his purse and pulled out a huge wad of naira. My eyes popped out of my head and he laughed. 'Forget it,' he said. 'You didn't just turn rich. It's the currency. You won't get as much for it as you think.'

I grabbed the bundle and my room card and stuffed it into my rucksack. When I kissed him on the cheek, a couple at the next table stared and the woman frowned and shook her head.

People thinking Dad and me were a strange sight

obviously hadn't changed. My cheeks burned at what the woman might have been thinking.

When I stepped into the street, my belly did somersaults. I was actually in Nigeria. How freaking unbelievable was that?

I smiled at the heat, at the sun crashing down and the frenzy of the main road. The traffic was loud, like in Lagos, with hawkers, bus conductors shouting and the smell of smoke, food, spices and oil wafting through the air. Even the green slime in the gutters couldn't kill my mood. I had seen so many colourful African fabrics that my jeans and monotone tops suddenly seemed boring. I needed to find something more Nigerian to wear.

'Sista, it is hot! Buy cold drinks,' a girl called from a kiosk, holding up a Fanta.

'Thank you, I'm fine,' I replied with a wide grin.

The word 'sista' had me smiling like a goof. She thought I was one of them! My brown skin, darker now from the summer sun in England, fitted in perfectly. Yesterday, it was Dad who'd received the attention. People had called him *Oyinbo* which meant 'white person' or 'foreign person'. Dad stood out, awkward and pale, and I went completely unnoticed.

I hurried towards the large sign of the mall further up the road, keeping to the cool shade of a fenced area of trees and staggered to a halt beside a pair of tall wrought iron gates. In the distance, Olumo Rock perched grey and overpowering in the middle of the city. Chilly winds whispered across my arms and up my neck from inside the thick iron bars. A wide driveway framed by dusty green bushes led to an imposing building that looked out of place on the modern street. It was three storeys in the colonial style, with columns, arched lintels above its doors and countless windows, and a balcony wrapped all the way around.

Bronze letters danced before my eyes.

Olumo Haven – Day and Boarding School.

I could feel the words calling out to me urgently. Olumo's peak towered behind the letters and a warm feeling trickled through me. I felt connected to the rock, to the very ground I was standing on and to everything around me. This was where I was meant to be.

A single thought repeated itself, again and again. *I cannot go home.*

9

Feeling like a traitor, I slunk back to the hotel an hour later to find Dad lying by the pool.

'Got this from the hotel shop,' he said, holding up a book called *The Secret Lives of Baba Segi's Wives*. 'It's really good.'

'Oh, so you are beginning to feel the Nigerian vibes,' I said, sounding more carefree than I felt. 'Check these out!' I placed my hands at my waist and posed, wagging my head. I had found a lovely Ankara hairband with bright red and yellow African motives and huge loop earrings with Nigerian map shapes dangling from them. He gave me a thumbs up and I threw myself on the lounger beside his.

'So, what are the plans for today?' Dad asked.

'We can chill if you'd prefer,' I said.

'I want to know what your plans are. We are here because of you and I am at your service, my little Nigerian girl,' he said, and winked.

I grinned. I wanted to try calling myself 'Nigerian girl' later when I was alone.

'I would like to go to the National Identity Management Commission to ask about Jimi,' I said, avoiding Dad's eyes. I knew it was a wild goose chase and he thought so too. But I had to start somewhere. Maybe Jimi wasn't a common name in Nigeria. It was probably short for James or Jakob, but we only needed to find those who originated from Abeokuta or who lived here – it would be like searching for that famous needle in the haystack but it wasn't entirely impossible.

～

We came back disappointed. The lady at the commission had not been forthcoming. 'I am sorry, but I cannot give out private information, even if your case does seem … erm, touching.' When she saw my face, she added, 'I will try to help you find your biological father.' She shot a quick glance at Dad, then passed us a card. 'Call this number in two weeks and I will see what I can do.'

While waiting for a taxi to take us back to the hotel, some children dressed in rags begged Dad for money. They ran after him, chanting a song, calling him *Oyinbo* and giggling. Dad had not spoken since. I could feel the question hanging on the tip of his tongue. *Is this how you feel back home?* There was pain and understanding in his eyes, but I had looked away. Angry that he had to experience being the outsider before realising how I felt. I slammed my rucksack in the corner of our room.

'I have changed my mind, Dad. I want to do a school exchange year,' I blurted.

'Oh,' Dad said, confused at the sudden outburst. 'Has the Nigerian experience woken your sightseeing genes?'

I shrugged. 'I guess so.'

'Come here,' he said, and pulled me into a hug. 'I am happy we did this. I know how important it is and I am really glad to be sharing it with you.'

I leaned into his hug and felt my heart melt towards him. I had to work harder not to blame him for things that weren't his fault.

Dad seemed to be feeling emotional as well because he held me tightly.

'It hasn't been easy, Tara. We wanted to do our best,' he said, letting go of me. He stared at his hands.

'What do you mean?'

'We wanted to be good parents. We worried that other parents, parents who look like you, who know what it feels like to be you … that they might have done a better job… I'm sorry if we weren't always the best…'

'Dad…'

'But when we saw you that first time, you were so tiny and sweet … we fell in love with you.'

To my horror I saw he had tears in his eyes.

'Oh, Dad!' I grabbed his hand. 'You and Mum did a great job. I have never wished I had other parents. Please believe me.'

I caught his eyes and he looked at me, uncertainly.

'All this...' I waved my hand around the hotel room. 'Coming here, to Nigeria. This has nothing to do with *us*. It's about *me* – finding myself, my roots. That's all.'

Dad nodded, a weak smile building. 'We are proud of you. Your mum and I really want the best for you. We want to support you any way we can. Okay?'

I nodded, feeling closer to him than I had in a long time.

I fell back on the soft hotel bed.

'So, school exchange, yeah?' he asked.

'Yeah,' I said slowly. 'Would you and Mum allow it?'

'Well, it's a bit late now, you're about to go into your GCSE year...'

'Dad, please! I can repeat my final year in the UK. I'll work hard to catch up, I promise...'

Dad scratched his head. 'I'm really not sure, Tara. Maybe we could still find a school willing to take you for a couple of weeks. Which country were you thinking? Germany? USA?'

I sat up, nervous now. 'No. I want to do the free-choice option in a different country and organise the trip myself. I want to do a year!'

Dad stiffened as he realised where the conversation was heading. He shook his head. 'No way!'

'But why, Dad? You and Mum always said an exchange would be a great idea!'

'Yes, a school-organised exchange programme for a couple of weeks.'

He raised his hands. 'I am not going to discuss this with you.'

'But why not? You still haven't answered my question.'

'Because it's preposterous! You're only sixteen. I'm not leaving you alone in this, this...'

I folded my arms across my chest, heart pounding angrily. '*This* place, Dad ... is my home.'

He cringed and I felt like slapping myself for hurting him.

'It's the country I originate from,' I added. But the damage was done.

Neither of us spoke for a while.

'Look, Tara, Nigeria is a third-world country. It is dangerous. They have malaria!'

'Against which the doctor gave us drugs! I would be careful and always use mosquito repellent spray.'

'They have cholera and who knows what else?'

I rolled my eyes. 'In the far-off villages, Dad! Where there is no running water!'

'They have kidnappings and terrorist attacks.'

I snorted in exasperation. 'In the north, hundreds of kilometres away. It didn't stop us flying over, did it?'

'Yes, but we are on holiday!' Dad retorted, spit flying from his mouth with the force of his words. 'For a week!' He was pacing the room. 'Have you been planning this all along?'

'No, Dad! I swear. It's just … there's a boarding school down the road. That's how I got the idea. Their term starts next week. I checked their website. Can we take a look at it, Dad? Please? It seemed really nice.'

Dad stared at me with wide eyes. 'I can't believe you are doing this. We actually got tickets and flew here. Wasn't that something?' He walked into the bathroom and slammed the door.

I grabbed the pillow and pressed it to my face. The thought of what I was doing to Dad and Mum worried me. But the thing twisting my insides was fear of leaving. I couldn't go back. I would not. Here was where I belonged.

10

I pulled out Ruth's little blue diary from my rucksack. Even though the random words and unfinished drawings still didn't make sense, opening the book steadied me, each page pulling me further in. I grabbed the pen from the desk and flipped to the last entry. I could continue her story by including mine.

Thoughts poured from me. Shaky feelings that hit the page in hot bursts. My jumbled words screened out the distant calls of night hawkers, the low hum of music from the poolside bar below, Dad thrashing in the bath. Each slash of the pen was like a tiny knot loosening inside.

When Dad came out, my hand was hurting. He looked like he'd let too much shampoo into his eyes.

'You have changed, Tara,' he said finally, his voice a quiet rasp. 'Since that night you woke from your dream, screaming, I feel...' He sighed. 'You are so different, it's like I don't know you any more.'

I closed the book and held it to my chest.

Dad was staring at me as if I was another one of those Nigerian meals. Too foreign, too weird.

Anger flickered inside me, sparking within seconds into a full-blown flame. Why wouldn't he try to understand?

The air tensed. Dad must have sensed it too because he frowned and looked warily over his shoulder. Cold air seeped into the room, wrapping itself around us. I hugged the book more tightly.

Dad began shaking his head wildly. 'I don't... I can't...' he mumbled and rushed to the window, tearing it open and clawing at his throat as he gasped for air.

'Dad?' I asked, my anger sizzling away into fear.

A roar gathered in my ears, like a whirlwind was right in the room with us. Dad clasped his hands to his head. He could hear it too.

'Dad!' I cried again.

Silence fell and he glanced around the room, rubbing his temples like he was seeing it for the first time.

Slowly, with distant, tired eyes, he faced me.

'We should call your mum.'

My stomach dropped. With Mum joining the conversation, my chances would be even worse.

'Oh, okay,' I muttered, feeling dazed. I joined him on the bed and he dialled her number.

'Hon, we have a change of plan,' Dad said in an

unfamiliar voice. 'Tara will be staying here for a while. There's this great boarding school...'

'What are you talking about?' Mum thundered through his mobile phone. 'What is going on?'

I peered at Dad, trying to understand what was happening. This was not making sense. How had he changed his mind in a minute? Dad's tense face blurred as he continued speaking in his odd way and Mum screamed hysterically into his ear. A feeling of complete calm came over me and I realised it was going to happen.

I was going to stay.

11

Dad hugged me so close I was scared he would break my ribs.

I still could not believe it.

Hundreds of students and their parents bustled around the large hall of Olumo Haven. The air felt heavy, laden with the smells of people, bags and excited chatter. I breathed it in, savouring the familiar taste, like a déjà-vu. I wanted to touch the ornate columns, slide my hands along the walls and empty niches where statues had once stood.

Anything to get more of this long-lost feeling.

But Dad was holding me tight.

Only the smallest ones, juniors on their first day, looked like they wouldn't let go of their parents' hands anytime soon.

I loosened myself from Dad's grip.

'Are you sure about this?' Dad whispered.

'Yes, Dad!'

He had been acting so weird these past few days, looking lost and not speaking much.

Before I could say anything more, he let go of my hand, turned and left.

I stared after him, surprised at his abrupt departure. *Nothing more to say*, I thought with a sigh. I was on my own, just like I'd wanted.

We had spent the last three days of our trip buying everything I'd need: school books, toiletries, black cotton underwear, simple brown shoes and the few private belongings that were allowed. The school provided the uniforms, bedding and everything else.

'Phone in here, please,' a broad woman standing at the luggage counter said briskly.

It dropped from my hand into the box with a thump. It felt like the last connection to my parents had broken away and a warm feeling of safety leaked out of my bones.

You can call them soon, I told myself. Normally phones weren't allowed, but Dad had arranged I could get mine from the hostel manager and call on weekends.

The woman noticed my trembling fingers. 'Is everything okay, dear?' She placed a pile of ironed grey uniforms on the counter. A sign read: *Mrs Abimbola – Hostel Manager*.

I nodded.

'This is your first day here.' She smiled, but while her lips parted showing teeth, her forehead remained stern.

'Yes,' I replied.

'It is, "Yes, Ma",' she corrected, rummaging through my things.

'This is not permitted.' She held up my joggers. 'This is not school wear. Is this your mufti?'

'No … erm … Ma. That's just to be comfortable in the evenings.'

She shook her head slowly, eyes slanted in disapproval. 'The school provides in-house clothing. You are allowed two sets of mufti to be worn for outings only.'

I looked wistfully at my comfy joggers, panic rising.

'No problem,' she said. 'It will be kept for you.' She wrote something on a list, and placed them, neatly folded, in the box with my phone.

◦━◦

A long, roofed walkway connected the main school building to the dorms, with tall, umbrella-like trees giving additional shade from the glaring afternoon sun. Its archways were made of a perforated brick and the trembling leaves caused a riot of light to scatter through. A gust of wind whistled through the branches like a thousand whispers. I stopped mid-stride and looked up.

The trees were just old: nothing abnormal about them. I took a deep breath. I had to get myself together. The rough nights had me more and more on edge.

I walked a little quicker, hauling my bags over my shoulders. Best find the dorms, so I could calm down and start settling in.

Mrs Abimbola had said there were three dorms: Amina, Buchi and Funmi, named after famous Nigerian women. My room was Funmi 14. I practised saying *Funmi* the way Mrs Abimbola had done – almost like *Foomi*, but in a slightly nasal way. The walkway opened on one side to reveal steps leading down to a square lawn with a sign saying: *Atrium*. Three dorms formed a U around it and I followed the sign to Funmi House.

A lump formed in my throat as I approached the door that said Funmi 14. I didn't know how to share space with a single sibling; how would I survive with five other girls?

Excited chitchat came from three bunk beds that crowded the room.

All were taken, except for the lower bunk beside the door.

'Hello,' I said, but no reply came. Since no one said anything, I dropped my uniforms on the empty bunk and pushed my bags towards the locker beside the bed.

The moment I dropped my things, the room went quiet. All eyes turned on me.

'What the hell do you think you are doing?' asked a skinny, hard-faced girl from the bed opposite. She had screwed open a bottle of nail polish and stared at me with heavily made-up eyes, nail brush poised as if in attack. The pungent smell of polish drilled into my brain.

I stood like a deer in headlights. All I could think of was Mrs Abimbola's words: 'No make-up, no jewellery and no nail polish.'

'Leave her alone, Lola,' the girl above me said. She was reading a thick, tattered book that looked like it had gone through the hands of every person at Olumo Haven. 'Were you assigned to Funmi 14?' she asked.

'Yes,' I said hoarsely.

'Well, she has to ask first,' the girl with the nail polish said. 'She can't just barge in, throwing her things around and taking up space.'

'I'm sorry, I assumed…'

'Don't go around assuming. How about courtesy and politeness?'

'Well, I didn't want to bother you, everyone seemed busy.'

Lola looked me over like she wanted to knock me down with a gust of her artificial lashes. Then the meanness left her and she stared at me warily.

'Is it okay if I take this bed which is the only one not occupied? And is it okay if I take this locker which is obviously not in use?' My voice was cold now. This was worse than I had imagined. But I wasn't feeling my usual longing to disappear. An angry whirlpool was brewing in my belly.

Lola burst out laughing. She laughed so hard she fell backwards on her bed. 'OMG. What kind of accent is that? Did you land here, like, straight from London?'

I turned my back and began stuffing things into the locker.

The girl in the bunk over mine clicked her tongue and hissed in a way I had never heard before. 'You are so rude, Lola. No home training!'

'Hey, watch your mouth, Bisi.' Lola jerked up and made the same hissing sound more loudly. 'What do you want to do about it?' She pouted her lips and rolled her eyes dramatically.

A girl who stood by one of the bunks chatting with the others, hurried out.

I continued folding my clothes into the locker, heart pounding and a sinking feeling in my stomach.

Lola began singing:

'Pussycat, pussycat, where have you been?
I've been to London to see the Queen.
Pussycat, pussycat, what did you do there?
I frightened a little mouse under her chair.'

'Goodness, I am out of here,' a tall girl in a bunk beside the window said. 'Halima, are you up for a stroll to the wall?'

'Sure,' Halima said and climbed down, a blue hijab draped over her head.

'Sure!' Lola repeated in a high-pitched voice. Halima did not react but followed with a roll of her eyes.

At the door the tall girl held out a hand to me. 'I'm Chidinma. Welcome to Funmi 14,' she said with a broad smile and the most perfect set of teeth.

'Thank you,' I said, warming to her friendly smile. Chidinma frowned and cocked her head, peering at me a moment too long. She looked like she wanted to say something, but let go of my hand and was gone.

What was that all about?

From the corner of my eye, I watched Lola carefully slide her freshly painted toes into flip-flops and get up. She was tall when she rose to her full size and wore baggy boyfriend jeans and a black T-shirt with the words, *No Shit!* written on the back. I wondered how she'd got in wearing it.

'Oya, Rosemary, make we commot for hia! Let's shake up the campus jareh!'

The girl called Rosemary glanced across and gave me an uncertain smile before following Lola, who bounced out of the room.

I slumped on my bed.

What had I done?

I could still run to Mrs Abimbola and tell her I'd changed my mind. Dad was on his way to Lagos now, but I knew he would come straight back.

I shook my head. *Stop being foolish.*

This was what I'd wanted and I wasn't going to be put off by one sour encounter.

I breathed in and exhaled deeply.

'Not a nice welcome,' a voice said. An upside-down head appeared and I jumped.

It was the girl with the tattered book, Bisi.

'Do not even begin to take notice of Lola. She has a serious inferiority complex and feels endangered when anyone prettier crosses her path.' Bisi winked, which was strange to see upside down.

I shrugged.

'What's your name?'

'Tara.'

'And was she right? About London?'

I shook my head. 'Nowhere so exciting,' I said. 'Further west and very countryside.'

'But you didn't just arrive, did you?'

I looked up sheepishly. 'Kind of.'

The girl's eyes widened.

'Less than a week ago.'

'Oh, wow, but it's not your first ever visit to Nigeria?'

'Well, kind of,' I said again with a grin.

'For real? Are you one of those wild, wayward kids of Nigerian immigrants who get sent home to learn discipline and respect? Because you came to the wrong place, girl! This private school is for softies and sissies,' she said with a slight snort.

I shook my head, wondering at her words.

'Are your parents Nigerian?'

I was about to say no when I remembered my biological father was – very likely – Nigerian. 'Well, ehm ... the answer is ... complicated,' I said, not meeting her eyes.

'Speak no further,' she said. 'I know what you mean. Complicated is *the* word to describe my life!'

Bisi, whose face was beginning to darken from the blood flowing to her head, gave me one more scrutinising gaze before disappearing.

Then two legs in jeans stepped down the ladder at the side of the bed.

'Come,' she said, slipping into flip-flops and heading for the door. 'I'll show you the campus.'

12

'Okay, so you'll need to know where to go for food, entertainment, and for sanity. And where *not* to go so you don't get into trouble.'

Bisi walked through the corridor of Funmi Dorm and stopped at a large room. 'This is the Funmi common room.' Some chatting girls lay sprawled on sofas and waved at Bisi.

'Hi,' Bisi called. 'This is my new bunk mate, Tara.'

'Oh, Funmi 14 has finally been filled,' said a lanky girl, chewing gum noisily. 'That bunk has been empty for a while.' The two others exchanged glances and looked me up and down.

'Hi,' I said, feeling like bacteria under a microscope.

'Welcome to Funmi Dorm, house of amebos and oversabis but nevertheless the best dorm,' the lanky one grinned.

'Na Funmi House dey reign!' another girl from the far corner of the room called.

I managed a quick smile, feeling overwhelmed by their Nigerian slang and curious stares.

Bisi dragged me along. 'Hanging out in the common room would be cool, but unfortunately it's beside Mrs Abimbola's room.' Bisi lowered her voice. 'I guess you met our hostel manager already. She is also our dorm mistress and when she is in her room, she likes quiet. As soon as someone laughs or raises their voice above a whisper she comes charging.'

We left the building and Bisi pointed back to our block. 'That was Funmi Dorm, as you know. This is Amina Dorm,' she said, pointing to the left. 'And that, opposite, is Buchi Dorm. Those are our two prep rooms. The prefects keep them under control, but if you want peace, as in, a place to be alone, you need to get creative. That's the one thing I hate. You are never truly alone. Even the bathrooms are half-open cabins, so you can't shower without seeing someone else's feet or ass and you can't sleep without hearing someone snore.'

We passed under the brick archway and came out on a large field surrounded by buildings and a fence with trees at the far end. Girls sat on benches talking and laughing excitedly. The arched walkway curved through trees and back to the old colonial building. It looked just as impressive from behind, with its balconies running across the back of the building.

'That's where we'll have classes?' I asked.

Bisi nodded. 'All classes, the reception hall, labs, teachers' and principal's offices are there.'

She walked in the opposite direction. 'This way leads to the dining hall. Dinner is at six-thirty. When I've shown you around, it will be dinner time and we'll have to change into our PUs.'

'PUs?'

'It's not official. PU stands for prison uniform. Our hostel wear.'

I raised my eyebrows.

She grinned, showing the cutest dimples. She was pretty when she smiled, though she seemed more of the serious type. This was the first time I'd seen her loosen.

'Because it's like a prison here?' I asked.

A shadow crossed her face briefly. 'Doors locked at eight, lights out at ten, bunk beds, fences and security? What does that sound like to you?'

She smirked at my worried expression.

'Don't worry, they're also called PUs because they're so damn ugly. Yep, enjoy your last moments in those jeans. Have you examined our hostel wear at all and observed the full magnitude of its hideousness?'

I shrugged and shook my head.

'They want us to feel ugly so we stop bothering about our looks and invest all our time in studying.'

I laughed and Bisi snorted.

'Oh my days! You will soon have the pleasure of seeing your sack-dress couture in pink-and-purple check.'

'That,' she went on, now pointing to the opposite side of the field, 'is the famous wall. It separates our campus from the boys'. Their campus is the mirror of ours. I don't know why it's called the wall since it's very obviously a fence, but, yeah. The boys also have a field on their side. They share the dining hall and school buildings with us, but they have their own separate entrances.'

She winked. 'The main action happens behind the trees at the wall. That's the number one hang-out spot for entertainment.'

We headed for the dining hall when a woman walked towards us.

'Good evening, Mrs Owoyemi,' Bisi greeted her.

'Good evening,' I said.

The woman smiled brightly. 'Welcome back, Bisi. How were your holidays?'

'Thank you, Ma, they were fine.'

'Okay, then, go on and settle in before the stress of school work takes over tomorrow!' The woman waved.

'Thank you, Ma,' Bisi called.

'Thanks,' I called.

'Add "Ma" or "Sir" after everything and you'll be fine,' Bisi said. 'That's an extra bit of respect that gets you far and keeps you out of trouble. Just a tip.'

I nodded gratefully, feeling awkward.

'Mrs Owoyemi is responsible for dorm housekeeping and supplies,' Bisi continued. 'She is very okay. Not one of the worst. If you need new sheets or run out of toilet paper or sanitary pads or toothpaste. That kind of thing.'

'Oh, okay.'

'What class are you in?'

'I think I'm in Senior Secondary 2B,' I said, remembering my admission letter.

'Oh, great, SS2B is my class,' she said. 'I can help you tomorrow.'

'Thank you,' I said, relief flooding me.

We moved on, passing a locked gate with a garden beyond. I moved forward, wanting to see more when the light changed, shadows obscuring the path and stretching into murkiness.

'Dusk comes so quickly here,' I said. Dad and I had noticed it. As if someone threw a blanket over the sky and darkened the world in an instant.

Bisi shrugged. 'It's the closeness to the equator. It makes sense to me. No reason delaying the inevitable end of things, is there?' Her teeth flashed and I saw a dimple. 'We should go back.'

The trees trembled in the breeze and strange whispers swished through the air. I cocked my head, feeling weirdly alert. 'What's over there?'

'The school orchard. Some pawpaw, orange and mango trees, and the school gardener has a farm. It's out of bounds, though; the gate is always locked.'

'Why?' I asked.

'Students used to work there as part of agricultural projects or as punishment. That was long ago. Then something happened and they put up the gate. That was before I came. Now it's forbidden.'

I leaned over, trying to see further into the garden. The play of shapes was eerie, seeming almost alive, shifting like in an old puppet show.

Suddenly something sleek and feline stalked between two trees and slunk into the thicket. It was so real, so large. I blinked and gripped the gate.

'Do we have cats on the grounds?'

'Hmm?'

'Like large … cats?' I faltered, feeling foolish.

'No animals allowed on campus,' Bisi said, looking back nervously.

There it was again. The swishing, whispering sound and a gust of chilly wind. A tremor shot through me as a distant howl rent the air.

I glanced at Bisi. But in that moment a loud gong rang out and Bisi began to hurry away. 'Are you coming? Dinner's in half an hour. We have to run.'

13

The prison uniform was as bad as Bisi had warned. Some girls had adjusted theirs and didn't look as ridiculous as I did beneath the huge sack-like dress. I sighed at the mirror before hurrying after Bisi.

Mrs Abimbola was standing at the dining hall entrance, closely watching the girls file in.

'Hey, Lola!' she called, hauling her out of line. 'What is this you are wearing?'

Lola's PU was extremely short and waist-hugging, revealing slim but well-proportioned curves.

'What do you mean, Ma?' Lola asked in a sweetly polite voice.

'Don't play with me, girl! You know perfectly well what I mean.'

'Oh, my dress, Ma? I had a growth spurt over the holidays. I was shocked to see it is now rather short, Ma.'

'Don't tell me your stories, Lola. If you come here with that dress tomorrow, you'll be in serious trouble.'

'Okay, Ma,' Lola said, still sounding cheerful. 'Obviously, since I am such a good seamstress, I'm sure I'll have fixed the dress by morning.'

Mrs Abimbola seemed ready to swipe Lola off the face of the earth. Lola didn't cringe; she just swung around and swayed into the hall.

I huddled close to Bisi, happy she had offered to go with me and even happier that my dress was well below my knees.

But when it was my turn, Mrs Abimbola folded her arms and the sides of her mouth went down even further, which didn't seem physically possible. 'Why haven't you fixed your hair yet?' she asked sharply.

'Ehm…' I swallowed, nervously checking the crowd forming behind us.

'So sorry, Ma,' Bisi said. 'I was supposed to weave it before dinner, but I had issues with my luggage.'

Mrs Abimbola eyed Bisi, then me and finally nodded. 'Okay. But next time weave your hair before you arrive at school. You know what little time you have with all the settling in on arrival.'

'Okay, thank you, Ma,' Bisi replied, nudging me.

'Y-yes, thank you … Ma,' I stuttered.

'Thanks,' I whispered, stumbling after Bisi into the hall.

I almost turned right back. The hall was filled with boys and they were all watching the door to see who was coming in. As a new student, I was getting a lot of stares. My fingers went down to my dress. It was pretty clear now that it did matter how the PUs looked. My afro was not helping either. Only now did I realise that every single girl's hair was in neat corn rows. *How had that escaped me?*

I hurried to catch up with Bisi. She seemed popular; people waved and smiled as she wove through a crowd of kids, hugging and chatting excitedly. I joined her in the queue where food was being shared out. Spicy scents wafted through the dining hall and my belly rumbled. A row of men and women clanked loudly with metal spoons and large dishes. They worked fast, dipping and dishing, their white uniforms already dotted with the bright green and red sauces they slapped on to plates. I stared at the strange white chunks one of the women had dropped on to my plate. She pointed at two sauces and looked at me expectantly.

'Both,' Bisi said, nudging me.

'Yes, both,' I said quickly.

'That way you have an alternative if one thing tastes terrible. The cook here is into experiments.' She rolled her eyes. 'One day your stew may be perfect, next time he might put in some ginger-lemon or minty-spice mix that will ruin your day and maybe your night. Every day is a surprise.' She cast a wry glance at her own plate before heading towards the tables.

I eyed the thick white slices swimming in sauce.

'Hey!' a boy called from a window seat overlooking the field. 'Ahn, ahn, my favourite girl ever is back to school.' Bisi smiled a wide one and hugged him. He was tall and dark and … the only word that came to my mind was 'hot'. One of those sporty-looking guys you would expect in the school athletics team. His house uniform, which was green for the boys, fitted him perfectly. But it was his eyes that made me self-conscious. Large, warm and deep.

He noticed me and I quit staring, almost letting my tray fall.

'This is Tara,' Bisi said.

'Hi, I'm Lanre, nice to meet you,' he said with a friendly smile that made my insides tingle. If there was something I wasn't used to it was male attention – or any attention at all.

I managed a grunt and a half-smile and sat beside Bisi.

'So, how were your hols?' he asked her.

She shrugged. 'All right, I guess,' she said in a low voice. 'I spent exactly two weeks at home. The rest of the time I was at my aunt's, out of everyone's way and being useful by helping with her brats.' She spoke quietly through clenched teeth. I avoided glancing over, not wanting to be caught listening to an obviously private conversation.

'Sorry about that,' Lanre replied and patted her hand briefly. He sounded so intimate I wondered if they had a closer relationship. 'Well, I won't lie, I'm happy you're back. I was hoping you wouldn't convince them to let you go back to day school in Lagos.' He smirked and Bisi boxed his arm.

'There was no chance, so here I am back in this hellhole!' She sighed and turned to me. 'Sorry, I didn't mean that, Tara. It isn't that bad. It's just not my personal choice to be in boarding school, that's all.'

I nodded, not sure what to think.

'My parents sent me here in the middle of last year, and I didn't find it very funny.'

There was an awkward silence. 'So, how were your holidays, Lanre?' Bisi asked in a lighter voice.

'Oh, very okay,' he said. 'Quite lazy. Chilling with friends, video games, Landmark Beach and cinema. You could have come with, you know, instead of being by yourself,' he added, nudging her.

Bisi shook her head. 'Don't forget I wasn't by myself, I was with the brats! But you know me, Lanre, I'm perfectly fine if I have my books and tons of series to watch.'

We attacked our food and fell silent. The thick white slice was actually manageable when eaten with the sauces. Lanre turned to me. 'So, first day of boarding school ever? Or just first day here?'

'First ever,' I replied.

He raised an eyebrow. 'Where do you come from?'

I sighed. My accent was going to give me away each time.

Someone leaned across our table, pressing close and pushing their chest into Lanre's face. He moved back to see who it was.

My belly cramped when I saw. Lola.

'Hi, Lanre,' she said in her fake sweet voice. 'How have you been? I can't believe I am back in this godforsaken place. Countdown, two more years to freedom!' She sounded over-excited and girly, waving her hands about as she spoke.

Lanre looked surprised, but smiled.

'Oh, you've met London, I see? Bisi's new playmate, huh? What's up with the hair, London? Do we have a new lawbreaker in town?'

'She has a name,' Bisi cut in.

'Chai, don't be so stuck up, Bisi. London doesn't mind.' Then she stalked off.

Lanre shook his head and Bisi twisted her lips and made her hissing sound. 'Don't mind her,' she said. 'She's not worth the waste of one single thought.'

'Tara is not even from London,' Bisi added, turning to Lanre.

'So where are you from?' he asked.

'My, ehm ... Dad's Nigerian and I ... decided to do an exchange year.' I quickly grabbed my glass to avoid looking at them.

'So how are you finding Olumo Haven?' Lanre asked, and I was grateful to him for changing the topic. He smiled and I could see he understood I didn't want to elaborate.

'Oh, it's exciting, like an adventure. It's all new, just like this strange slice of a thing on my plate.'

They burst out laughing.

'That's yam,' Lanre said. 'It grows as a big tuber underground.'

'And you'd better like it, because you are going to be seeing much more of yam. It's like the Yoruba national food,' Bisi said.

Lanre nodded gravely. 'Yoruba people hardly eat anything else. You will soon know it in all its forms. Pounded yam, yam porridge, fried yam, amala, boiled yam, yam pepper soup, yam balls, yamaritas...'

My eyes widened as he ticked them off on his fingers.

'Each of these can be combined with soup or stew or vegetable so the number of yam dishes you can have for breakfast, lunch and dinner are actually infinite.'

I choked and began to cough and Bisi handed me my glass. The piece I had tasted was all right. I could imagine eating it once in a while. But three times a day was a lot.

They burst out laughing, almost choking themselves. I folded my arms across my chest, trying to fight the impulse to laugh, before I joined in.

14

The little girl fell on to a flat ledge of rock. She tried to stand, staggering, as if she could hardly hold herself upright. She sobbed and sniffed as she climbed higher. The sun fired down and sweat gathered on her forehead, seeping into the corners of her eyes. In one swift movement, she wiped the sweat with the back of her hand, dried it carefully on her red wrapper and continued to climb.

'No,' she mumbled between gasps. 'No, please, no.' She pulled herself up through dark crevices, around sharp-edged boulders, only stopping briefly to catch her breath. She knew her way. She had done this many times before. A sudden rush of dusty wind blinded her. She wheezed and shielded her face. The Iroko tree towered above, roots buried deep in the rock.

'Why did you not protect us?' she cried. 'Why did you not help?'

A dark thing swelled in her chest, so strong she thought she would burst. Her entire body began to tremble, as if there was an earthquake. Shifting her foot to get a better hold, she heaved herself over the last ledge.

With the tip of the faded red cloth wrapped around her small body, she cleaned off the sweat and tears. Her dark skin and closely shaved head were covered with red dust, as if she had rolled in the dirt. Hurrying to the far edge, she ignored the gunshots and smoke and cries of horror below. What she was searching for was further away.

The trail of dust was moving fast, leaving the burning huts and thatched roofs far behind and heading for the thick forest ahead. She could discern the horse and a faint silhouette of the man leaning forward, as if protecting something.

As she lifted her head and raised her fists towards the sky, she wailed, '*Iiieeee ... Jiiimmmiii!*'

━

I woke screaming.

'What the—' someone croaked, and I recognised Lola's voice.

Darkness. Tall, four-post structures surrounded me. Where was I?

Then Bisi was there, laying a cool hand on my hot forehead.

'It's all right,' she whispered. 'It was just a dream.'

15

A loud thump, like a stick hitting metal, crashed through my veil of sleep. It was still dark. My heart beat fast, not because of the sound, but because of the dream. It felt like I had spent the entire night trying to reach the girl on the rock. Again and again I had climbed, struggling to keep up and when I had finally reached the top, gasping and breathless, there she was, arms outstretched. Each time I tried to touch her, to ask about the dust trail in the distance, about Jimi, she disappeared.

Bisi groaned from above.

Lola made a hissing sound and covered her face with her pillow.

Soon after, two shadows got up, rustled about and left the room. Bisi came down slowly. 'We should go shower,' she whispered. 'The earlier the better, if you don't want to queue.'

Like a zombie, I followed. Without Bisi, I would have been lost. I watched her in the mirror as we brushed our teeth. She looked as tired as I felt. Hot blood rushed to my cheeks at the memory of her patting and hushing me like a baby. Goodness, I was so embarrassing. She had been unbelievably kind since I arrived. I hoped she wasn't put off, but this morning she hadn't looked bothered by me trailing after her like a lost puppy.

'We have to fix your hair,' she'd said after dinner yesterday, like it was the most normal thing. She'd sat on my bed, placing my pillow on a newspaper on the ground between her legs and pointed. 'Sit,' she'd said, and began gently combing out my hair.

I glanced at my new look in the mirror and touched my corn rows. I couldn't help smiling at the feel of my neat plaits. I loved how Nigerian I looked.

'Are you coming or do you prefer to spend your day in front of the mirror?' Bisi called from the door.

I jumped back, feeling foolish, and saw her grin as she slipped from the bathroom. We were the last, apart from Lola, who had strolled in like a queen after everyone else, and was still humming under the shower.

The dorm was empty and I hurried after Bisi.

Darkness had only just retreated, leaving cold, grey streaks behind. The morning air was heavy, but fresh, and I would have preferred to stay outside than squeeze into the crowded prep room. Mrs Abimbola was up front giving orders in a much-too-loud voice. Otherwise all was quiet, the atmosphere sluggish.

'What are we doing?' I asked Bisi as Mrs Abimbola began chanting a tune.

'Morning prayers,' Bisi whispered.

Everyone joined in the songs of praise. I looked down at my fingers feeling more self-conscious than if I had been the only one singing. Dad and Mum weren't regular church goers. Prayers in Nigeria might as well have been magical incantations. They sounded just as strange. Most girls had faraway looks or closed their eyes as they sang. I looked up and stiffened. Mrs Abimbola was scrutinising me, her eyes sharp. I moved my lips, pretending to sing. This felt more than stupid.

'Now, let us all say the Lord's Prayer,' Mrs Abimbola called. *Ah, finally, something I know.* I almost cheered and recited it with more fervour than I had ever felt before.

'Bloody stupid sheet!' I yanked at the ends of my bed for the twentieth time. Why couldn't I smooth it out and stretch it tight the way the others had?

'London seems to be having difficulties,' Lola

sneered. 'Don't you want to ask your school mother to help you?' She looked up at Bisi.

'Why don't you mind your business and make your own bed for a change?' Bisi said.

'Why should I when I have grateful fans who want to show me their love?'

I glanced at the scared-looking junior struggling with Lola's bed. She had done a better job than me, though.

'Is it all right now?' the girl asked, looking ready to cry.

'You can go,' Lola told her, without even a thank you and the girl scurried away.

After prayers, Mrs Abimbola had warned she would be checking the rooms. 'I will not condone any disorderliness,' she had repeated, her eyes two fierce slits.

Lola leaned against her bed post and turned to me. 'London, sure you can cope? An ajebutter like you? I mean, nightmares and screams after just one night away from Mummy and Daddy?'

'Oooh, Lord,' Chidinma hissed. 'Lola, it is too early for your beef. Leave the girl alone jareh!'

A knock on the door and Mrs Abimbola marched in. Every girl jumped in front of her bed, looking as nervous as the junior that had just left. I stood where I was, frozen stiff.

Mrs Abimbola's hands were folded behind her back. She nodded at Lola and Rosemary, then continued to Chidinma and Halima's corner. A small piece of PU stuck out of the locker beside their bed. Mrs Abimbola pointed a finger without speaking. Halima hurriedly thrust the uniform back in. Then she discovered something like dental floss on Chidinma's bed and found a bra beneath her bunk. When she reached my bed, she shook her head solemnly.

'Tara, this is not how to make a bed. Tomorrow I expect better.'

She stepped on the first rung of the ladder and inspected Bisi's bunk.

'What is that book?' she asked Bisi sharply. 'Let me see.'

Halima and Chidinma exchanged a look and Lola smiled mischievously.

Bisi climbed up to get it. Mrs Abimbola studied the cover, then nodded and gave it back. 'If I ever see any of those godless romances, you girls will smell pepper in this dorm for a week. Have you heard me?' She tugged her ear fiercely, her head swinging towards us so that each of us could see.

'Yes, Ma,' we answered and I was surprised at my automatic reply. I was adapting well.

'No one is going astray under my watch! You will all behave and be good examples for the younger students!'

'Yes, Ma,' we chanted again.

'Hurry up for breakfast and have a good first day of school, everyone,' she said and left the room.

I slumped on to my bed, then jumped back up, staring at it in shock.

Bisi giggled. 'Relax, there's only one inspection per day, no sweat.'

School was in a loud buzzing uproar. Day students arrived through the front gates, joining the boarders in a frenzy of greetings, hugs and excited chatter.

Someone swayed into SS2B. I groaned. Lola! Luckily, she ignored me and was busy chatting with a guy at the back of the class.

Bisi gave me her timetable and I quickly copied it into my exercise book. First subject Monday morning was Yoruba. That was going to be tough! I didn't mind learning a new language, but everyone had either spoken Yoruba since they were kids or learned it in school over the past four years. I was going to be a freaking beginner among experts.

When the teacher, Mr Bolaji came in, Halima, Chidinma and some other kids hurried out.

'Why are they leaving?' I asked Bisi.

'They don't do Yoruba,' she replied. 'Halima is going for Hausa class and Chidinma for Ibo.'

'We actually learn all these Nigerian languages?'

'Well, only the three main ones. No chance of you learning the other two hundred.'

My eyes widened. 'Two hundred languages!' But my awe was swept away in the rush of Yoruba whirling past my head. I felt transfixed the moment Mr Bolaji began to speak. He was a smallish man with large friendly eyes and a teddy-bear face.

The class remained as rowdy as before, everyone calling out melodious replies in Yoruba and laughing.

Then the class went quiet and I stiffened as everyone stared at me.

Mr Bolaji spoke in English. 'I just said, we have a new student in class this year. What is your name?'

'Tara Walther,' I replied.

'You are welcome, Tara Walther. How good is your Yoruba?'

I heard a loud snort from behind.

'I don't think they do Yoruba in London,' Lola said with a nasty giggle.

'I am not from London,' I said, louder than I had intended. 'Unfortunately, I do not speak any Yoruba.' My skin prickled with all the eyes watching me.

'Hmm, let's see,' he said, scratching his head. 'We haven't had this situation before, but it shouldn't be a problem. I will bring you the JSS1 lesson book and some easy exercises next time. You will not be able to follow our course yet, so I will give you additional exercises to do during class. Maybe we can squeeze in an extra lesson here or there. Are you a boarder or a day student?'

'A boarder,' I replied.

'Even better. Then you can always ask your fellow boarders for help if you have questions.'

I nodded, wanting the focus on me to end as soon as possible.

'I am sure her new school mother will be very willing to do that,' Lola chipped in.

'Will you back off, Lola! What the hell is your problem?' Bisi hissed.

'Ahn, ahn … can we calm down, please? Everyone, bring out your textbooks.'

He switched back to Yoruba and I instantly felt a hazy sensation wrap itself around me. Even though I didn't understand what Mr Bolaji was saying, the rhythm of the words felt softly familiar. They cradled me like an old lullaby, rocking me gently and burning the tip of my tongue, as if I could almost hum along. I was sure, as I was of my own name, that I'd heard the melody before.

16

'Action at the wall oh!! There's a party happening!' Chidinma's head disappeared from the door of Funmi 14 as quickly as it appeared.

Bisi jumped down from her bunk where she'd been reading as usual and grabbed my arm. I was ironing my uniforms for the next week.

'Come on, leave that,' she said, pulling the plug from the socket. 'Saturdays are fun days – they're what make boarding school endurable!'

Bisi had said that twice already since waking up. The day had started early at seven-thirty a.m., but after waking at five-thirty for the entire week, this was like a soul massage. Mrs Abimbola had left us to ourselves and school prefects seemed more relaxed. Even though there were chores and assignments to do, I could feel in my gut Saturdays were going to be my favourite days too.

'Are you coming?' Bisi called. I looked up at the clock. Three p.m. Two more hours and it would be time for phone calls. My belly twisted at the thought of speaking to Mum and Dad. Especially Mum.

Pushing it aside, I hurried after Bisi. She was running, almost skipping, with excitement, and I felt her thrill seize me as I ran after her, giggling. She had brightened since that first day, becoming much more talkative. We'd spent literally every moment together.

A girl was kneeling on the overgrown lawn in the atrium, cutting grass with a machete. I slowed down, shocked to see how wretched she looked. Her PU was soaked in sweat from the blazing afternoon sun. I recognised her from Funmi Dorm.

'What is she doing?' I asked Bisi in a whisper.

'She is cutting grass.'

I rolled my eyes. 'I can see that! But why is she cutting grass in this heat?'

'Punishment.'

'Oh.' I looked back at the girl. She wiped sweat from her forehead and hid her face when she saw me staring. Her eyes were red and swollen.

'What did she do?' I whispered, feeling awful for her. Everybody passed through the atrium, it was so public.

Bisi shrugged. 'No idea.'

'Does she have to cut all of it?'

'No, I don't think so. You usually get a portion assigned.'

'Usually? Does this happen often?'

'Well, not often, but once in a while. You'd better work harder on your bed-making skills or you know what's coming.'

'Are you serious?' I stopped walking.

She laughed. 'Just kidding. You'd have to commit a worse crime to get this punishment.'

'Like what?'

'I don't know. Stealing or worse, being caught making out with a boy, or reading those romance books Mrs Abimbola hates so much.'

I giggled. 'I can't believe making out or reading romances is the same level as stealing.'

'In Mrs Abimbola's world, definitely!'

'What are those books, anyway?'

'We have lots hidden away all over the dorm. Everyone reads them. I can organise one for you, if you want?'

'Oh my goodness, no!' I said in horror.

Bisi burst out laughing.

'Are you that prudish?'

I prodded her playfully. 'You know full well what I mean! I don't want to get into trouble. I can't risk my life for some cheesy love story!'

'You have to get bolder if you want to survive around here, my dear! Living by the rules leads to extreme dullness, and if exercised continuously could lead to death by boredom!'

I giggled.

'Are the books indecent?'

'No, not really. Most contain mild sex scenes and have stupid plots about women falling for chauvinistic guys and getting their hearts broken. At the end they find out the men are not chauvinistic, but quite nice after all and they live happily ever after.'

'That's it?'

'Yes, and they are Mrs Abimbola's worst nightmare!'

We howled with laughter.

'They are good for information, though. So if you change your mind because you need to know how to go about certain things, tell me.' She bobbed her eyebrows meaningfully.

'I know all there is about the theory. It's the practical part I need help with.'

Bisi grinned. 'Whom are you telling?'

She glanced up and down the arched walkway, crossed it and peeked into the field. 'Okay, looks empty,' she said and grabbed my hand.

We hurried across the field, up to the benches where we stood around pretending to be talking. I could already hear music and laughter from behind the bushes. Bisi scanned the field.

'No dorm mistresses in sight. Quick, now!'

The weeds around the fence had been trampled by previous visitors and we squeezed through easily.

Ahead of us, between some shrubs, I saw a group of girls, Chidinma and Halima among them. They were dancing to quiet, rhythmic music. It came from a phone on the other side of the fence where some boys were standing. Two of the boys were dancing the same steps as the girls, swaying slowly. The others were talking in hushed tones and giggling.

'Hey!' One of the boys raised his arm and waved. It was Lanre.

'What's up?' he said, placing a fist between the gaps in the fence.

'All good,' Bisi said, placing her fist against his. He smiled and then we touched knuckles.

'Bisi, good, you are here!' Chidinma called. 'Please come and tell Ifeanyi the gist that Mrs Ogundipe told us. He doesn't want to believe me.'

Bisi disappeared and left me standing there. I stared at her back, panic rising at being left alone with Lanre. I could feel him watching me.

'So how was your first week?' he asked, looking the very opposite of how I was feeling.

'Good, actually.'

Breathe, relax! I told myself.

'Sounds like you were expecting worse?'

'Well, things have been quite new and I hardly had time to adjust.'

'Was it a sudden decision to come here, then?'

I nodded and bit my lower lip. I had said more than I wanted to. But his eyes were so sincere, so deep and dark, that I found myself disclosing more. 'I am on a journey of self-discovery. Searching for my roots.'

He raised an eyebrow.

'I … I was adopted and recently found out I have Nigerian family.' I lowered my voice.

'That sounds tough, I mean, not knowing and all.'

I shrugged.

'So, are you liking what you've discovered about Nigeria?'

'It hasn't been so much yet … but yes.'

'Well, then, we have to exponentially increase your discovery levels as soon as possible,' he said lightly. 'From what I know, yam has been ticked off your list.' He wriggled his eyebrows and I burst into giggles.

'How was your meeting with ogi and akara for breakfast this morning?'

'Akara is top,' I said with a thumbs up. 'But ogi was a disaster,' I said, remembering the sour, whitish pudding. I turned my thumbs down.

He laughed and something quivered in my belly. Was there a scientific explanation for how laughter could ripple through air and wire fences causing weird sensations in your body?

'Okay, right now you will be initiated into the world of Nigerian music. Unfortunately, at low volume due to

… ehm … the fact we're hiding behind bushes. Nigerian music is usually served loud as that brings out the spice. But, know you are listening to one of the kings of Nigerian music. No other than Wizkid himself!' He raised his arms and began swaying his waist, bobbing his head and singing along.

'Can you feel this hot beat?' he asked. He scrunched up his face as if the music was drilling into him.

I nodded with a grin.

'Come on, Tara, tell me you dey feel am!'

I raised an eyebrow at his switch to pidgin.

'You have to reply: yes, I dey feel am.'

'Yes, I dey feel am,' I said.

'All right,' he said and clapped his hands together. 'Then show me some waist, girl.'

I shook my head vigorously.

'No need to be shy. Allow your Nigerian roots to take over.'

'No way,' I said.

'Hey, give my your hands,' and he slid his fingers through the fence.

I looked at him, suddenly nervous. His eyes were earnest and his smile so reassuring I slipped my fingers into his.

'Nobody is watching,' he said softly.

I glanced sideways. He was right. The others were engrossed in something one of the boys was showing them.

'Just let the groove take control.'

I almost giggled, but saw he meant it. He closed his eyes and began moving to the beat and I found myself doing the same. The feel of his fingertips against mine was hypnotic. For a few seconds I was overcome by the music.

When the song ended and I could hear the laughter and chatter, I opened my eyes and found him staring at me. I grinned, loving the slow warmth churning in my insides.

17

'Tara, my love! Oh, I am so relieved to see you,' Mum cried. Her voice was shrill and I cringed at the sound.

'Hi, Mum,' I said, balancing my mobile on the window sill of the phone room.

'Peter! Come quickly, it's Tara!'

Mum's face was red, her eyes filled with tears.

'How have you been, honey?'

'I'm fine, Mum! Really! Everything's wonderful.'

'Oh, I am so glad to hear that. I've been … worried!'

Dad placed a hand on Mum's knee but she brushed it away.

Why did I feel so far away? So disconnected? Shouldn't seeing Mum like this make me more upset? It was as if the distance between us, the vast stretches of land and ocean had diluted my feelings. More than anything, I felt relieved they couldn't come and get me.

'Tara, listen, the minute anything goes wrong, and you don't feel good about this … the moment you want to come home, just call.' She cast an angry glance at Dad. 'I mean it, Tara. I will come and get you myself.'

'Please don't worry, Mum, I'm perfectly fine. I'm very safe in school – we aren't allowed to leave campus. I'm having a great time. I'm working hard as well; I promise I'll catch up when I'm back.'

'I'm sure you will, Tara,' Mum said with a sigh. 'I am proud of you, believe me. Even though I'm still mad at your dad. It's been tough not being able to call to check you are okay and having to wait till Saturday. I've spent all week on the internet reading about the school, looking for reviews and learning about Nigeria…' Mum placed a hand to her mouth, fighting tears.

'Your hair is amazing! You look so different,' Dad cut in.

'Thanks, Dad.'

Mum nodded, her lips trembling.

'How have you been? How is the food? Is it … are you all right?' Dad continued.

'Dad, it was you who found the food too spicy and the weather too hot, remember?' I laughed. 'I am fine and the food is great.'

'I really am glad to hear things are okay,' Mum said again. 'I was worried we would have you crying on the phone that things have been awful.'

'Mum! I am fine. Really!'

She took a deep breath. I could see she was struggling.

'You look grown up,' Dad said.

I felt overwhelmed by the conversation, and by Mum, and quickly changed track. 'How is Lulu?'

'Oh, she's missing you,' Mum said. 'Come here, Lulu.' She patted her thigh and a fluffy red bundle jumped on to her lap. 'She keeps lurking around your door and spends the nights in your bed.'

'Hey, Lulu,' I said, but the cat buried its head in Mum and didn't react.

A sharp knock behind me startled me. The door swung open, hitting the wall.

An angry-faced Lola burst in. 'Your ten minutes were up five minutes ago!'

'One more,' I called, waving her out.

But Lola folded her arms across her chest, and stood defiantly in the doorway. Nosy girls in the queue peered into the room.

'Dad, Mum, I have to go. Please don't worry. I'm okay,' I said quickly.

'Promise me,' Mum said in a panic. 'Promise, if you don't feel good about anything, anything at all, you'll go to the principal's office and get permission to call home and be picked up. We can be there in forty-eight hours. I've checked the flight connections.' Mum's voice grew louder with every word. I tried to lower the volume, but her voice resounded like a shrill megaphone. I felt a growing anger in my chest against Lola, and an even bigger rage boiling up at Mum's words.

I wasn't going to promise anything. There was no way I was going to allow anyone to take me back.

Even though Mum was waiting, I replied in a flat voice: 'I'll be fine, don't worry.' Then switched off my phone.

18

'What is your problem?' I yelled at Lola. My face was in hers and my chest was heaving. I didn't even know when I had crossed the room to stand in front of her.

'Everyone has ten minutes, okay? Not ten for us and fifteen for London!' She pushed me hard and glared. My back hit the door and the anger drained out of me as quickly as it appeared. I glanced at the girls in the queue. One was shaking her head and the others were whispering. I felt ashamed by my outburst.

'Look, it was an emergency and, by the way, no one told me I only had ten minutes.'

'Well, of course no one told you,' Lola sneered. 'I guess Big Daddy London settled that with some British pounds.'

'What?' I cried. The queue of girls watched me like a jury in court.

'Yes, same way he arranged for you to have your mobile for video calls while we have to use the landline. You think you are better than us, with your London and your accent and your British pounds.'

'Heh?' Tears blinded me. No other words would come. Dad and the principal had arranged I could use my mobile since the landline was too expensive to call the UK. Hot shame burned my face at how arrogant I must seem, like a spoiled brat whose dad had bribed everyone to make her more comfortable.

'What's all this I am hearing?' Mrs Abimbola's voice pierced the silence. 'Lola, have you gone mad? Are you accusing the principal of taking bribes? Both of you in my office, right now!'

'But I'm next in line!'

'Right now!' Mrs Abimbola's words were dangerously low.

Lola sawed through my body with a wicked roll of her eyes, before marching off, rage sparking from every pore.

I followed slowly. The anger had left me empty and weak. Behind me, Mrs Abimbola spoke to the girls.

'Nobody gets bribed in this institution and nobody gets special treatment. Have you understood?

'Fifteen minutes of video call sounds like special treatment to me,' Lola called.

'Will you get into my office now!' Mrs Abimbola

hissed. She faced me, hands on hips. 'Did you make a fifteen-minute video call?'

'Well, I didn't check the time because I wasn't aware we had ten minutes and—'

'Was it a video call?' she interrupted.

I nodded, deflated. 'Mrs Abimbola, I didn't know it wasn't allowed.'

A junior girl in the queue imitated my accent, laughing at how I pronounced Mrs Abimbola's name. My face quivered and a new wave of frustrated tears burned my eyes.

—

'Lola, I am deeply disappointed in you,' Mrs Abimbola began as soon as she closed the door of her office. 'Tara is a new student and instead of making her feel welcome or advising her if she makes mistakes, you attack her in front of everyone.'

Lola stared straight ahead, her face rigid.

'Where do your parents live, Lola?'

Lola looked up, irritated. 'Ibadan.'

Mrs Abimbola nodded. 'Does that not sound very comforting? They are just two hours away. If you are ill or if anything happens, God forbid … they are close by. On visiting day, in a month's time, am I right that your parents will be here?'

Lola shrugged stiffly.

'Tara's parents live thousands of kilometres away, on a different continent. She has no single relative in the whole of Nigeria. How does that sound in comparison?'

Lola scowled at the desk without replying.

I cringed at Mrs Abimbola's words. I hoped I *did* have a relative somewhere in Nigeria. If not, then I wasn't sure what the hell I was doing here.

'Do you have anything to say, Lola?'

Lola shook her head, arms folded. Mrs Abimbola sighed.

'You, Tara?'

'I am terribly sorry, Mrs Abimbola.'

I could feel Lola's eyes shoot invisible nails at me, but I went on. 'In future I will set a timer to keep to the ten minutes and I will only use the call function without video.'

Mrs Abimbola nodded.

'You can go, Tara. But I don't want to hear talk of favouritism in this dorm again, so make sure you are up to date with all common practices. If you don't keep to the rules, you will be punished like everyone else.'

19

The tunnel was dark. The girl had to lower her head as she stumbled forward. It was tight and uneven, sometimes widening, sometimes only large enough to crawl through. The shadow lurked, always a few paces ahead, moving with stealthy, supple steps. The tunnel grew bigger and she ran into a high cavern, her heart beating erratically. There were breaks in the ceiling, through which dim streaks of light trickled. The girl searched frantically, but it was difficult to see anything clearly. A sudden movement caught her attention. Cat-like eyes watched from a corner of the cavern, then disappeared into another tunnel.

'Duro! Wait!' she called, hurrying after it.

A feline shape prowling in the tunnel further up stopped her. Head cocked, eyes narrowed, the shadow was gliding along the stone wall, soft spotted fur brushing the rock. It was coming for her.

The girl screamed and its roar blended with hers to become one and the same.

~

The spine-chilling sound reverberated through the tunnels, through my head.

'Stop it! Quiet … shhh.'

I covered my ears.

'Bisi, shut your abiku friend up.' Lola's voice cut through my dizziness.

My eyes cleared and cold crept up my limbs. I was standing barefoot in the corridor in front of Funmi 14, my hand on the door handle. Bisi appeared from the darkness of our room. She placed a hand on my arm, loosening my grip on the door.

'I am okay,' I hissed, shaking her off me. Stumbling into bed, I grabbed my pillow with trembling fingers and covered my face.

~

What is an abiku?

I wrote my question on a slip of paper and pushed it across the table towards Bisi. She stared at it for a while, then looked up to where Prefect Cynthia sat in the corner of the prep room. Prefect Cynthia was leaning over her book, forehead creased. Students often called her Perfect Cynthia, because everything about her, from her grades to her white socks, carefully trimmed nails and starched PU, were perfect. She was so busy cramming for her final year exams that all she cared about was silence and never noticed if chairs were empty or anyone was missing.

Bisi began packing her books together, nodded her head towards the door and tiptoed out. I grabbed my own pile of books and whizzed after her. My learning session had been useless, my mind endlessly wandering back to my dreams.

'Goodness, I couldn't stand the stuffiness of that room a minute longer,' Bisi whispered as we hurried through the atrium.

We dropped our books at Funmi 14 and slipped from the dorm unnoticed.

Bisi looked round and pulled me through bushes to the back of the building.

'How, for heaven's sake, did you ever find this place you are taking us?'

Bisi laughed. 'Don't worry, when you have spent some weeks here and feel like you will explode if you cannot have one minute to yourself, you will understand.'

We reached a tall fence and began walking alongside it. A wide river gurgled beside us and almost seemed to be following us as it curved around the fence.

'That's the Ogun River,' Bisi said.

Beside us the unruly bushes transformed into neat rows of corn and ahead stood a grove of fruit trees.

'Wow, I've never seen an orange tree!' I said, stretching out to touch the yellowish-green fruit. A sharp pain tore through my hand.

'Careful! They have thorns,' Bisi warned too late.

'Yeah, just found that out,' I murmured, sucking my finger. 'This is the garden with the locked gate, right? The one we're not supposed to be in?'

'Yes, which the school gardener takes care of. He is the one person we might meet, so watch out.'

I peered warily into the orchard, remembering the strange shadow I had seen on my first evening. It looked different now, the trees growing in neat, clear formation. And yet ... I felt uncomfortable. The late afternoon sun drew long lines, cutting sharply into the lighter spaces. Now we were out of the shade and in the open, the sun beat down mercilessly. The air was thick and damp. Was it the proximity to the river? I closed my eyes briefly to steady myself. The scent of citrus fruits filled my nostrils: a fresh, tangy smell, followed by an afterthought of rotting sweetness. I shuddered.

'Are you coming?' Bisi whispered.

I scurried after her, past a weird tree with fat greenish fruits huddled like greedy piglets at their mother's breast. Large leaves on long stems shot from the top, unlike anything I had ever seen.

'Pawpaws,' Bisi said, catching my expression.

'It's like the Garden of Eden, serpent and all. Just without the apple tree.'

Bisi grinned.

'What's this for?' We passed a pile of metal rods and planks thrown together carelessly beside two mounds of grainy sand. They looked out of place beside the well-kept garden.

'They were going to build an additional dorm. The boys' dorms have been made larger. Only two boys share a room. But shortly before construction of the girls' dorm, weird things happened and they lost some female students. So they abandoned their plans.'

'Really? What kind of weird things?'

Bisi shrugged. 'When I first arrived I hardly spoke to anyone and didn't care about the stuff I heard. Things like the place being haunted.'

'What?'

Bisi snorted. 'It was hysteria. All boarding schools have ghost stories. Some kids took it seriously, called their parents to take them out. The principal panicked and stopped construction until things settled. That's why six of us share one small room, even though this is supposed to be a posh private school for rich kids.'

She sounded angry.

'Not that I'm a rich kid,' she added. 'I'm here because my mum was sent to a horrible boarding school, where food was disgusting and never enough, and sadistic seniors brightened their days by punishing juniors, sending them on useless errands like personal assistants. She felt guilty about having to send me to boarding school and chose the best one she could find. She shipped me off and out of her way.'

'You sound upset with her.'

I was shocked to see Bisi's eyes fill with tears. She didn't reply, just shrugged and pointed in front of us. We were approaching a rock about three metres high, roughened around the edges with a smooth, flat top that sat right in the middle of a fence.

'My secret place!' Bisi announced. She walked to one side and pulled her PU up to her waist, exposing our compulsorily black cotton underwear. Wedging her foot into the fence, she yanked herself up, finding a crevice in the rock for her other foot and a few seconds later she was lying on it.

'Oya, your turn, Tara,' she called.

I followed her example and climbed up.

'Lie down quickly,' she said. 'So we're not visible from staff quarters.'

It was lovely up on the rock – totally private and serene. A large tree shielded us from the school buildings and I could hear the river bubbling below. Flat on our bellies, we edged forward towards the river. The water whirled past in an endless ripple of sparkling green. We watched in silence. Only the splashing of fish and the breeze rustling through the trees stopped me from falling asleep.

'This place is the best,' I said after a long while.

'But it's a secret, okay? No telling anyone else.'

I nodded, pleased she'd shown me her special place.

'Everything all right?' I asked, thinking of her outburst earlier.

She nodded. 'I am just annoyed with my mum, that's all. Yesterday, she told me she probably won't be making it on parents' visiting day. Last year she didn't come either. We live in Lagos, for goodness' sake, not Sokoto! Lagos is an hour and a half away! "I'm so sorry, dear, the association of estate ladies fixed their annual whatever ceremony on exactly that date! And you know, as the chairlady, blablabla".'

'What about your dad?' I asked.

Bisi snorted. 'He's always away on business and doesn't really care.' She traced the uneven lines of the rock with her fingers. 'Sometimes I wonder, why bother having children if you don't have time for them? I mean, it's not a written law, is it? It's just that primary instinct in living things to reproduce. But we should be above that! We are not animals!'

I thought of Ruth. Why did she have me? Had I been a mistake? An unplanned burden she hadn't been able to cope with?

I pushed a loose piece of rock over the edge and watched it bounce and disappear. No plopping sound followed. Instead, it hit something underneath. Propped up on my elbows, I stretched forward and saw a dark hollow beneath us.

'There's a cave of some sort under here.'

Bisi nodded. 'Yes, it's overgrown, though.'

I tried to see through, but couldn't. Suddenly, my skin prickled with a feeling of being watched. But it came from above, far away. I twisted round to search the sky. Thankfully the sun was beginning to tire. Then I saw in the distance a huge mound of majestic grey overlooking the city.

'Wow, we can see Olumo from here!' I cried.

'Cool, right?' Bisi said.

I instantly felt the connection and drew a long breath.

Bisi glanced at me. 'You shouldn't let yourself be bothered by Lola and her friends, you know. She is never happy if she isn't centre of attention and she obviously feels threatened by you.'

'But why? I haven't done anything to take attention from her, apart from the fact I am new.'

'And from England … and absolutely foreign with your accent and all … and pretty … and Lanre likes you.'

'Yeah, right,' I said, my ears heating up. 'I'm sure Lanre does not *like* me like that.'

'Oh, you haven't noticed? Why do you think he always comes to sit with us at lunch?'

'Because he is *your* friend?'

Bisi shook her head. 'Yes, his dad went to school with my dad, so we are sort of family friends, but he would only come over once in a while before. We never used to hang out *all* the time … until you came.'

'Oh,' I said, feeling shy, and instantly high that Lanre liked me.

'Is it okay? I mean, you don't, ehm…'

'Have feelings for Lanre?' Bisi laughed loud. 'Oh, no, not at all. I have seen him cry, like snotty-cry when he was little, and have done sleepovers at his place. He is like a brother to me.'

I let out a sigh of relief.

'Even though he's like a brother, doesn't mean I don't know how hot he is,' Bisi said with a wide grin that made her cute dimple deepen as if it was grinning along with her.

'He is!' I said with such energy I felt giddy. 'He doesn't have a girlfriend, right?' I was nervous, finally spilling the question that had been on my mind from the first day I met him.

'Nope! And I can tell you, friend to friend, he is a really sweet guy.'

'So, who have you thrown your eye on? Anyone in particular?'

'Well, yes, a friend of Lanre's actually. Theo. I'm trying to get Lanre to hook me up. But he is so annoying about it, trying to do some big brother-type talk, about how he is almost eighteen and he's not too sure about it. The only unfortunate thing is Theo is Lola's cousin.'

'Oh! Yes, that *is* unfortunate!' My smile faded at the thought of Lola, and Bisi nodded.

'The beast of Funmi 14.'

'Well, I don't blame her for calling me weirdo and abiku, whatever that means.' I glanced at Bisi. Unlike with Maxine, I was beginning to feel grounded with Bisi, enough to share my fears. But I was scared of what she thought of me. Of what she might say.

'I know I'm a mess with my nightmares and screaming at night,' I said quietly.

'It's not your fault,' Bisi said. 'Everyone has nightmares and should be able to relate.'

I thought of Chidinma's pitiful look at breakfast and cringed. I didn't want to be the poor weirdo everyone pitied.

'Do you want to talk about them?'

I stiffened. 'What does *abiku* mean?' I asked instead.

Bisi sighed. 'It's difficult to explain to someone who didn't grow up here. Abikus are spirit children who come and go from our world as they please. They hurt their parents, causing pain.'

'What do you mean they come and go?'

'They are born into a family, then die young and are reborn to the same parents, again and again. They are cursed, because they are never truly in this world and are always being called by their spirit family.'

'What?' I sat upright and stared at her, not believing what I heard.

Bisi sat up as well, her gaze on me.

'Hey, you aren't meant to believe this myth. I only wanted to explain it to you. It doesn't have anything to do with you! No one thinks you are an abiku.'

I kept staring at her, my mind racing.

'Hey, Tara, listen, abiku is an insult. Do you get? It doesn't mean anything.'

'But why does Lola think I am one?'

'She doesn't *really* think you are! She said it because of the nightmares and because she is mean. According to the old tales, when abikus are called by their spirit family, they faint or have visions or nightmares, so they can meet them.'

I thought of my nightmare and how the girls in my room had woken to find me sleepwalking and screaming at the door. Tears burned my eyes. I slid backwards letting myself down the side of the rock, stretching my hand towards the fence. Somehow I missed and found myself slipping and all I could hear was Bisi's scream.

20

I landed in a painful heap, the fence breaking my fall. As I examined my scraped knee and ripped PU, I noticed something coppery gleaming from between tufts of grass at the foot of the rock.

It was a round pendant with a loose clasp where it had broken from its chain. Tiny symbols were cut into it and in the heart of the symbols, a face formed – two eyes, sharp and cat-like. The eyes coloured and deepened. For a brief moment, they took on a piercing shade of green, the symbols becoming dark spots and the round pendant assuming a golden glow. My heart began to rush its beat, blood hurtling through my veins. My ears buzzed with the pressure and a distant echo rang through the noise.

Tara!

Bisi was calling me. I jerked up, startled out of my thoughts as she clambered down the rock.

'Oh my goodness, Tara, why didn't you reply? I was so scared you'd hurt yourself.'

Crouched on all fours, I slipped the pendant into the pocket of my PU.

'I'm fine,' I whispered, still feeling dazed.

I sat up, wrapping my arms around my knees to hide my trembling fingers.

Bisi scanned the orchard to make sure the gardener wasn't in sight before seating herself on the ground opposite me. 'What is this all about, Tara? Talk to me.'

I had never even told my parents what I dreamed about, but now it felt like my fear had broken the dam holding me together.

I told her everything.

Absolutely everything.

It felt like a huge relief. Bisi didn't say a word until I finished. She was watching me closely, looking stunned. I could understand: it was a monstrous story.

'So you have visions about the past?'

I nodded.

'And you saw Olumo Rock in your dream before you knew what it was, and you knew about the house on the cliffs before you went there, and how your biological mum died? You really see things?'

I nodded again warily, my hands in tight fists as I waited for her to jump and run.

But she just took a deep breath. 'Okay, everything

has a logical explanation. So, you have visions. There has to be a reason why. We have to find out what it is you are meant to see, where this is heading. Then I'm sure everything will be all right.'

I looked at her doubtfully. 'What if I am an ... abiku?' I found it difficult to say the word. 'What if the spirits want me to join them? I don't want to die young, like my ancestors.' My voice was a whisper.

'You are not going to die young,' Bisi said firmly. 'First of all, abikus are a Nigerian phenomenon. They are not even a phenomenon, they don't exist! But the point is, your ancestors, the ones who died young, are European! That doesn't make sense.'

She stared at me, waiting for a reaction. I sighed.

'Secondly, if any spirits call you and want you to come, then all you need to do is say, "No, thank you very much, I am happy right where I am."'

She got up and began pacing around. 'First thing we should find out is if the Identity Commission has information about this Jimi person. If he is your father, he probably has an explanation for everything. The identity commission won't open on Saturday when you have your phone. So we need to ask a day student if they can lend us their mobile to call them.'

I nodded, relieved to have a plan. But doubts filled my mind. Shreds of my dreams flashed before my eyes. The little girl climbing the rock. Had she not called

Jimi too? Or was I mixing things up? Where was the connection? What did all this mean?

'Then, and this is more difficult, we have to get you to Olumo Rock,' Bisi went on. 'Maybe Lanre can help us. From what you said, the rock seems to be the key to everything. You have to go to Olumo again and ... talk to it or listen to it or feel it!' She waved her hands around as she spoke, as if talking and listening to a rock were the most natural thing in the world.

'But I was there already! Apart from some visions, nothing happened.'

'Yes, but your visions are somehow connected to Olumo and they seem to be taking their time and coming to you gradually. If you want to know more, maybe you should trigger them.'

I began to feel more hopeful. 'Thanks, Bisi ... for not laughing at me.'

'Oya come, jareh.' She dragged me up, pulling me into a tight embrace.

I hugged her back and a thought crossed my mind. 'Bisi?'

'Hmm?' she asked, still holding me.

'How do we get to Olumo? We aren't allowed to leave campus.'

Bisi let go of me and smiled mischievously. 'Well, that's the part where our plan gets complicated.'

21

'Should we still go to the fence before dorm gates close?' Bisi shouted above the noise of the showers and girls gossiping as they brushed their teeth. We had just come in from dinner.

I thought of seeing Lanre and a jolt went through my belly. I definitely felt like seeing him, and we needed his help, but I was scared of telling him my bizarre story.

'Lanre was heartbroken we didn't have dinner together,' Bisi said, grinning at me in the mirror.

'Yeah, right,' I said, heat rushing to my face. He had waved and smiled from where he'd sat surrounded by friends, but he definitely hadn't looked heartbroken.

'Well, you didn't see him staring at you because you had your back to him. I'm surprised he didn't burn a hole through your PU.'

I snorted and rinsed my mouth. 'I really should go to the prep room and do some serious learning,' I said.

Apart from wanting to delay telling Lanre about my weird self, school was beginning to be tough and it wasn't easy keeping up.

Bisi groaned. 'Don't be such an efiko!'

'I also have all these anthems to learn. The Nigerian national anthem, the school anthem, Funmi House anthem. You guys have an anthem for everything. I'm surprised room 14 doesn't have an anthem. Goodness, Nigeria is such a singing country!'

Bisi almost gagged on her toothpaste.

'Mrs Abimbola is on my case about the prayers and songs for morning devotion that I cannot sing.'

'Sunday *was* a disgrace,' Bisi said, still giggling. I rolled my eyes as she convulsed with laughter. On Sunday, the bible study teacher had asked me to strike up a song and I had stared at her blankly. 'Any song of praise at all, it doesn't need to be a hymn or psalm,' she had said kindly, trying to help. But that made things worse, because I didn't know a single one. I'd just stared at her with panicked eyes and a half-open mouth, like a bird that never learned to sing.

'The Nigerian anthem is so easy,' Bisi said. 'After a couple of times you will know it.' She dropped her toothbrush.

'Okay, join me,' she said, and began to sing at the top of her voice.

'*Arise, oh compatriots, Nigeria's call obey...*'

'Bisi!' I whispered, giggling. 'We can't practise in the bathroom!'

'Why not?' she cried. She straightened her back like during assembly and placed her right hand across the towel at her chest and went on even louder.

Someone hissed from a cubicle, 'Who is that? Stop disturbing, jareh!'

But then, one after another, girls' voices joined in at top volume. The whole room was vibrating with enthusiastic singing and every time we finished we started over, until I actually knew the words. We came out of the bathroom mid-chorus and almost stumbled into Mrs Abimbola. She shook her head in disapproval, but an amused smile twitched at her mouth.

'Calm down, we don't want any injuries. No hurrying in the corridors with wet slippers, please!'

Bisi and I stumbled into Funmi 14 like two damp, yelping puppies. Lola was alone and I saw her quickly push a book under her pillow. She hissed and left the room.

Bisi winked at me, placed a finger to her lips and pulled out the book. 'Let's see what the beast is reading.'

The title, *Jane Eyre*, was almost unrecognisable.

'Oh, I've read *Jane Eyre* too,' I said.

'Sorry, but there is no way Lola is reading that. Wanna bet?' She hooked her little finger into mine, then cut through our connected fingers with her other hand.

She grinned when she saw my bewildered expression and pressed the book into my hand.

'Open and see.'

After the first ancient pages they became crisp and white. My eyes widened. 'There's another book in here. Wow, Lola is such a sly one!'

Bisi laughed. 'That's how we all read forbidden books.'

'*The Seven Husbands of Evelyn Hugo*,' I read.

'Oh!' she said, raising her eyebrow in alarm.

'Why, what is it?'

'This one is dangerous. I'd heard a copy was circulating. Do seven husbands sound very Christian to you? Even worse, there's homosexual relationships in there! But it's an amazing story, you should read it when Lola's through.' She grinned when she saw my look of terror.

'I have enough trouble in my life, I don't need more,' I said, remembering Mrs Abimbola's horrific prayer yesterday.

May the Lord keep us from going astray, from having evil thoughts, from evil spirits, from being the devil's advocate, from being lesbians.

'What's Mrs Abimbola's problem, anyway? How can she be so publicly homophobic?' The first time I'd heard Mrs Abimbola, I thought I'd imagined it. But then she repeated the words and no one had found it strange. 'Shouldn't she be reported to the principal or something? Her prayers are discriminatory.'

Bisi snorted. 'Goodness, Tara, you are in Nigeria! Don't say that out loud. Welcome to the nasty side of your roots. Nigeria is homophobe country number one. The constitution does not condone homosexuality. You can go to jail for it. Mrs Abimbola is the executing body of this law in here.'

Suddenly we heard footsteps. Bisi snatched the book back and slid it under the pillow, just as the door opened and Lola returned.

22

'Are you girls for real?' Lanre cried when he heard our plan. His normally smooth, cute face was scrunched in a frown.

'Shh!' Bisi hushed him, glancing nervously at the kids by the fence.

'No way, Bisi! I'm supposed to be like your big brother, protecting you and all that, and you come to me with this wild idea!'

'Who the hell said I need big brother protection?' Bisi asked with a roll of her eyes. 'I can take care of myself, thank you!'

Lanre crossed his arms, and if I hadn't been so worried about what he'd soon think of me, I would have found him sweet.

'Hello-oh,' he said. 'Those were your mum's exact instructions. You were standing beside me when she said it!'

'I don't want to hear anything about my mum, Lanre, and I really don't need you lecturing me.'

'Secondly!' Lanre interrupted. 'If you didn't need a caretaker, you wouldn't be standing here asking for the impossible!'

Bisi grabbed my hand and yanked me away.

'You know what, thanks for nothing. It wasn't for me, but for Tara. She needs us, and I can't believe you would leave her hanging like that!'

'I, ehm...' I stuttered, frowning at Bisi to stop her harassing Lanre. She winked devilishly and marched ahead with exaggerated angry movements, dragging me behind her. 'We'll find someone else,' she called over her shoulder.

'What's all this, shakara? Will you stop making a show and come back so we can talk in a reasonable way?' he called.

Bisi's grip on my hand tightened before she released it and turned. She was trying to hide a grin and Lanre shook his head in exasperation.

'Okay, please explain why you girls want to scale the fence, risk the worst punishment, even expulsion, just to get to a rock.'

I sighed, realising I would have to give him more details.

'You can trust him,' Bisi said softly.

I looked around and when I was sure no one else

was nearby, gave him a quick summary of the situation. I had been staring at the fence, afraid to look into his eyes.

'Okay, you are more Nigerian than I thought,' he said when I'd finished.

I looked up gingerly. 'Why?'

He grinned. 'Well, you are straight from England and already into the highest levels of juju and superstitious stuff I ever heard.'

I couldn't help beaming at the way he smiled at me.

'Oya-oh!' Bisi grumbled. 'So, are you going to help us or not?'

He scratched his head. 'Calling the National Identity Commission is no problem. I'll ask Wale – he'll let you use his phone after school.'

'Is it really okay to ask him? I don't want to be a bother.'

'Don't even worry. He's a good friend and knows I like you a lot.' Lanre was watching me intently now. Our eyes locked and my whole body went kind of limp.

I gripped the fence. 'Oh,' I said, feeling more awkward than ever. 'Ehm, thank you.'

He smiled and I found myself smiling back.

'Oh god,' Bisi groaned. 'Is it really the moment for this cheesy stuff? We have bigger issues here. Lanre? Wake up! What about getting us to Olumo?'

Lanre's smile faded into a frown. 'That's the part I don't like.' He sighed. 'I wish there was a way we could do this during the day!'

'Yes, that's the problem. We've gone through all the options, but they don't give us more than an hour or two. That's too little time!' Bisi said.

'We thought of getting an excuse from Mr Bolaji for staying longer in class to practise Yoruba,' I said.

'Or one of us missing lunch by complaining about period pain, but they wouldn't believe both of us and it still wouldn't be long enough,' Bisi said.

'The chances of getting caught in the day are higher,' I added.

'You know how it is, there's no privacy,' Bisi said.

'It'll be tricky getting past security at the gate,' Lanre sighed. 'And even if we did, how do we explain our absence? It would be noticed immediately.'

'See!' Bisi said.

'Do you girls realise that not only do we have to break out of here, we also have to break into Olumo Rock? Because as far as I know they don't have midnight visiting hours.'

Bisi and I nodded. That had been giving us an even bigger headache.

'It's breaking the law! We could get arrested or shot, if someone thinks we're criminals and calls the police. We would get a criminal record if we survived!'

'Mehn, Lanre, when did you become such a sissy! You were so much more fun when you were eleven.'

Bisi turned to me. 'Do you know, I once had a sleepover at his and we walked two kilometres through traffic and dark roads at midnight to get to the wildlife park in Lekki because we wanted to find a real-live bush baby. They're nocturnal and we had to go at night but that didn't stop us!'

'That's different,' Lanre said. 'We weren't conscious of our actions and the consequences.'

'Huh!' Bisi said, whipping her head around and placing her hands on her hips. 'I think you were not so much of an ajebutter then.'

'Will you stop calling me an ajebutter! This is serious, okay? Mehn, I am the boys' hostel prefect, for goodness' sake. I have a rep and responsibilities!'

'Lanre, I don't want to put you in an awkward position. You don't need to do this,' I said.

He searched my eyes for a moment, as if trying to see into me.

'It's okay, let's do it.'

Bisi clapped and he raised a warning finger. 'We still have to figure out how to get past security! The entire front wall is lit at night. That's going to be difficult, if not impossible!'

We were silent for a while.

'The river!' I cried, remembering the little rock at

the fence. 'What if we go to your secret chilling place and scale the fence? We could walk along the river and follow it to town.'

Bisi hooted and gave me a high-five. 'That's it, my girl!'

23

'**O**uch!' Bisi yelped as she tumbled forward. I caught her, steadying her on her feet. The missing bar of the bathroom window, a well-kept secret in Funmi Dorm, was our escape route. A gap so small it had gone unnoticed by Mrs Abimbola, but wide enough to have given many a wayward student before us certain liberties.

'Quick, stop dreaming around,' Bisi whispered. She grabbed my hand and we stumbled through the dark like thieves, scanning the shadows carefully as we moved towards the little rock at the fence. I could already hear the rush of the water. The air was heavy with the smell of weeds and fish, stronger now than in daytime.

I hoped all would go to plan and Lanre would be at the meeting point. He'd not sounded too worried about getting out of the boys' dorm; as hostel prefect he had access to the key. But he had to slip through the dining hall, the female campus and past staff quarters. My heart thumped anxiously. He would be in the worst trouble if he got caught.

At bedtime, when Bisi had winked at me with a sly grin, it had felt like an exciting adventure. Now, out between the shadows and the night, the full force of what we were doing hit me. This was no game. What if things went wrong?

As we reached the fence there was a sharp tug in my insides. Olumo loomed in the distance, its rounded presence pushing into indigo-grey sky. I stepped out from the bushes, twisting over the fence and around leafy branches to look. A cold wind swirled up from the open river, carrying a heavy, fishy moisture. I shivered, the familiar urge filling my limbs. I could hardly wait.

Bisi let out a burst of breath and I saw Lanre's tall shadow approach. I relaxed a little.

Silently, with Lanre in the lead, we climbed through the space between the rock and the fence. Soon we were balancing along the thin ledge beside the river, holding on to the fence for dear life and threading carefully around the undergrowth.

No one spoke. Occasionally there was the sound of yelping as one of us struggled.

The whole situation was so surreal I kept having to check Bisi and Lanre were really there and I wasn't dreaming.

'Careful,' Lanre whispered, breaking the silence. 'There's a rock sticking out here.' The river seemed to rush past faster, the cold night wind hurtling the ink-black water forward. Falling in would mean being swept away in seconds. We'd put the torches in Lanre's rucksack to avoid being seen. I felt my way, fingers groping for the solid pole that held the fence. Where was the moon when we needed it?

We warned each other of branches sticking out, or of holes in the ground, now speaking more freely as we left the school buildings behind.

'Mehn, the mosquitos are wicked tonight!' Bisi hissed and a loud slapping sound followed.

'The beasts can sense we can't use our hands to protect ourselves. Relentless devils!' Lanre replied.

The talking calmed me, relaxing my stiff muscles and I moved more smoothly. The others seemed to feel the same, because soon we had made good progress.

'Is the main road in sight yet?' Bisi asked for the upteenth time.

'No, it is not! Stop whining and asking that every minute,' Lanre hissed.

I grinned, enjoying the way they were always at each other like siblings.

Then, my foot caught in something tough, like a root. I slipped and my left foot skidded down the muddy bank. I yelped as ice-cold water filled my trainer.

A strong arm held me, stopping me from reeling. It was Lanre. I grabbed his shoulders, gasping from shock, as he pulled me out of the freezing water.

'Everything okay?' came a muffled voice out of my hair. I nodded, enjoying the brief safety and warmth of his arms.

The smell of river grass and fish was replaced by something fresh and citrus. Lanre's scent. I breathed it in slowly then stiffened as I realised I was in the tightest embrace I'd ever been in with a boy.

'Oh, ehm, sorry, I mean, thanks. That was close,' I said, placing my hands against his chest to push myself away.

He didn't release me and I was aware of my hands on his warm chest. My legs wobbled at the feel of him.

'Yes,' he said in a low voice. 'That was very, very close.'

I caught his eyes in the dim light. He was flirting, scanning my face with a lazy smile.

'Good god, are you guys for real? It is past midnight and we could get caught any moment, or worse, fall into this nyama-nyama river and you can only think of being all over each other? Oya, oya, move! This is not the time!' Bisi hissed from behind.

Lanre loosened his grip with a sigh and I reached out awkwardly to get a hold on the fence. My cheeks flamed and an even hotter feeling rushed through my insides as I glanced at Lanre's tall figure moving in front.

Finally, we got to the main road, still busy with passing cars and a group of people chatting near the school entrance. We hurried in the other direction, my shoe making smacking noises and my left trouser leg soaked up to my bum.

Lanre waved down a taxi.

'Good evening, Sir,' Bisi greeted when the car came to a halt. Loud music sprayed out of his radio.

'We wan drop near Olumo Rock,' Lanre said.

The young man eyed us like he knew we were up to no good.

'Oya enta!' he said.

'What if he recognises our PUs and calls the school?' I whispered, squeezed between Lanre and Bisi in the back.

'Shh,' Bisi hissed. 'If you shout any louder, he might hear you and do just that.'

'Like anyone would pick up a phone in school now,' Lanre said.

'I can imagine Mrs Abimbola sleeps with one under her pillow, ready for that exact phone call!' Bisi snapped.

'Do you know the way to the rock, Lanre?' I asked. 'What if he drives us back to school to hand us over?'

Lanre shook his head. 'Relax, Tara! This guy doesn't care who we are or what we are doing, as long as we pay our fare.'

But I kept glancing at the driver through his rear-view mirror. The ten-minute journey felt like an hour of torture. Creeping below the dorm windows and along the river had not seemed half as scary as sitting here, all exposed. Now we had a witness.

We got out on a street just before the entrance to Olumo Rock. Considering it was past twelve on a week night, there were lots of people around. Hawkers sat at the roadside selling akara and bread and roasted corn cobs, their faces made ghostly by flickering lanterns. We passed a group of rough-looking men sitting on downturned boxes and rickety plastic chairs in front of a kiosk. A radio stuttered music out of battered speakers. They eyed us lazily, puffing crooked spliffs, their smoke creeping towards us. Bisi tightened her grip on my arm and we moved faster.

We were so close now. The rock overpowered everything. I couldn't take my eyes off it, the lines on its face, its curves, marks, cracks and outgrowths.

My heart faltered to a flutter when we turned the corner. The road to the entrance, enclosed by high metal fences on both sides, was not empty. The gates at the end revealed two security guards. One was eating and the other was stretched out on a bench.

'Not looking good,' Bisi murmured.

'At least one of them is sleeping,' I mumbled.

'I have an idea,' Lanre said. 'I'll walk up and ask

questions. You girls have to find a way to slip past. Look, the gate is open.'

Bisi stared ahead without saying anything.

'Are you sure about this, Bisi? I don't want to get you in trouble. I would understand if...'

'We've come this far and I am not turning back now,' she said. 'Besides, this is the most exciting thing that has happened to me since I joined this stupid boarding school.' I saw her teeth flash in the darkness and I grinned back.

I turned to Lanre. 'I'm in,' he said. 'I just need a pen and a notebook. Wait here.'

He walked down the street to a kiosk that was still open and came back moments later holding a newspaper and a pencil.

'This will have to do.' He folded the newspaper so it looked like a notebook and walked towards the tall gate.

'Okay, Lanre, show us what you've got. You've got this, you've got this, you've got this,' Bisi whispered over and over.

Lanre walked up to the man in a slow, self-assured manner. The man was wearing a red baseball cap the wrong way around and chewing aggressively. His partner, wearing a white kaftan, lay still, unmoving.

The low rumble of Lanre's voice filled the quiet. What in heaven's name was he telling him?

Soon they were chatting like old friends. Bisi glanced at me and though I couldn't see her face clearly, I sensed her raised eyebrows. Lanre began scribbling things on to the folded newspaper, nodding his head vigorously as the security guard spoke. Lanre moved closer to the man, blocking his view of the road.

'This is it.' I grabbed Bisi's arm and we snuck along the fence, keeping to the shadows.

'August would have been the best time to come,' the man was saying. 'The shrine is only open during Olumo Festival. Just two people are allowed to enter. Our traditional ruler, the Alake of Egbaland, and the chief priest.'

It was almost too easy. Bisi and I slipped through, as we heard Lanre say, 'Really! Only once a year?'

'Yes,' the man went on. 'In the olden days they would sacrifice human beings at the shrine.'

The air was instantly electrifying. I could feel the rock on my skin, in my nostrils. Its closeness was overpowering, turning my body clammy and my heart, a mess of jumbled beats. I was going to get answers today; I could taste them.

Bisi bumped into me and gasped, covering her mouth.

'They sacrificed human beings?' Lanre asked, feigning shock. 'I have to write that down.'

He was really good.

'But that was in the past, sha,' the man said. 'Nowadays they sacrifice a black cow.'

My sight blurred as Bisi and I flitted across a circular space with a fountain, towards some steps leading up.

I had to sit down. My teeth were chattering, and the cold from my wet trouser leg was creeping up into my whole body.

'What's wrong?' Bisi whispered.

'I don't know.' I could still hear the security guard, but now a whispery sound mingled with his voice. A cold wind curled around me and I heard crackling, like a bonfire, calling me to come and warm myself. I grabbed the railing and my legs carried me up the steps to the first landing. I wanted to move faster, but my legs were slow to respond. I stretched out a hand to the rock, much too long before I actually felt it.

At the smooth coolness beneath my palms a half-stifled sigh escaped my throat. The crackling sound grew louder and I looked up at the branches bristling against the blue night. The guide had called this place the Panseke Garden on my first visit with Dad. The long, pointed seed pods cut through the sky like swords. It was the seeds that made the crackling *seke-seke* sound.

'We should hurry,' a voice whispered in my ear.

I stared at Bisi. My forehead drew tight. What was she doing here?

'I don't know how long Lanre can keep the guard occupied,' she said. Her voice was far away, like an echo.

I shook my head. 'No,' I cried and pushed her.

She fell backwards, her eyes wide, and the panseke trees beat their pods wildly above us.

'Tara!' she called after me. I stumbled forward, past the cowrie-decorated statues and the grave of a chief, wading through thick air. Then I fell down, out of breath, and a sour smell, slightly metallic like rusting iron, filled my nose. My hands felt slippery and dark marks stained the earth. I knew what they were before I looked up. Feathers trembled in the blood that was smeared on the shrine door.

The smell twisted my stomach. My limbs went limp and I felt I was being pressed to the ground. The sounds of the Panseke Garden became louder and louder, until it was an incessant drumming inside my head. I covered my ears.

Bare feet decorated with white chalk marks approached. The drumming became louder, wilder. They were coming closer, cowrie ankle bracelets rattling with each step. They were here for my blood! My heart raced and I shrieked, rolling out of reach.

'You can see it. I can see it in your eyes that you know!' a brittle voice said.

I gasped, searching frantically for the source of the voice. The drumming ceased abruptly and there she was in the shadow of the shrine. The frail silhouette of the old woman. The priestess I had met before at the top of the rock. Or was she?

I tried to speak, but my throat was dry. 'Good evening, Ma,' I croaked.

The silhouette was silent, though I could feel her eyes burning into mine.

'What did you just say?' I whispered. 'What do you mean?'

The clouds moved, and the moon shone through. Even though her face was obscured, I could now see the old woman was wearing a long red kaftan.

'I am looking for answers,' I said. 'Please!'

'Olumo is the answer. Olumo is always the answer. It is the end of our wanderings.' She spoke so quietly the words seemed to be inside my head.

'Follow me,' she said, and disappeared around the corner.

I jumped up, swaying slightly. I couldn't lose her.

She bent low to enter a cave and I followed her into the void. The air was musky and stale. There was a scratching sound and then a spark from a lamp. We were in a tunnel which went on into nothingness behind her. The flickering lamp made the walls eerily intangible: at once further apart, and like they were closing in. The woman seated herself on the ground beside the lamp. If this was the priestess, meant to be one hundred and thirty years old, she was extremely agile. I watched her untie a knot in the cloth around her waist and bring out cowrie shells and a stone. Sweat ran down my face, as the cold lost its grip on my body.

The woman began etching marks on to the floor. She had dropped the cowries beside her and I counted sixteen while she scratched a circle on to stone. When it was complete, she looked up. Bottomless eyes bore into me and though I could not make out their substance, her gaze was piercing, reading me.

When she spoke, I tensed, because of the strange way her voice slipped into my head.

'Your eyes are searching the places behind you. They are not facing the path that lies ahead.'

I swallowed as I realised what she meant.

'Your questions are of "who" and "why".'

I nodded.

She picked up the cowries and threw them into the circle. They bounced in a weird way, landing in all directions.

She frowned, muttering.

'A palm kernel must always have an inner core.'

The woman gathered them up and threw them. Again they scattered in an unnatural way. She shook her head, her hands hovering indecisively over the cowries.

Now I noticed something else. None of the cowries had landed inside the circle. It was large enough, and she had thrown them gently, and yet they had all bounced outside of the line.

My skin began to crawl.

She seemed agitated. Angry, even.

Then, the old woman moved her gaze from the cowries on to me. Her eyes were hollows, her face hard.

'A bottom must always have a top and an outside must have an inside.'

What did that mean?

'Half of you is empty. There is darkness in the emptiness. A wound. I see cursed souls lined up behind you. If you do not succumb, the line of cursed souls will grow longer.'

She made a sudden movement with her hand I could not decipher. My heart thrummed. Questions burned inside me.

'Tell me, please,' I gasped. My sight was blurring and she was fading. Or was I the one fading? I could no longer feel myself and I struggled to see her mouth, hear her words. And yet it felt so vital that I did. As she spoke, her mouth disappeared into the numerous wrinkles of her face and her face, like her eyes, turned entirely endless.

'I see you in front of a mirror. Soon, you will finally see and know yourself. The hole in your spirit will be filled and you will become whole.'

The light of the lamp began to flicker, then fade, and everything went dark.

24

Cold hands gripped my shoulders.

I screamed.

'Tara! What's wrong? Shhh!' It was Bisi, her voice panicked.

Why was I kneeling in front of the shrine? I stared at my hands in the moonlight – stained and dirty. I dusted a bloody feather off them.

'I'm fine,' I mumbled, letting her help me to my feet. 'What about Lanre?'

'We have a problem! A third person joined them and now the sleeping guy has woken.'

'Oh, man! What is Lanre doing?'

'He's still standing there.'

'We're never going to get out unseen!'

We hurried down, stopping in the shadows by the fountain. There was talking and laughter, and Lanre stood awkwardly, peering into the darkness. When the men looked the other way, I dashed out, waving frantically.

Lanre must have seen me, because he stiffened. Then, with a sudden movement, he grabbed something from beneath the bench and to my utter shock, started running.

Running as if the devil were after him.

At first the men stared in surprise. Then one of them shouted, 'Ole, thief! My torchlight!' and the men gave chase.

'Oh my god, Lanre!' I whispered.

'What the hell?' Bisi cried.

We glanced at each other, instantly understanding, and ran, like two horses gone wild. The slap of our trainers on the ground echoed in quick rhythm. We raced out of the street, halting at the corner, but Lanre and his pursuers were nowhere to be seen. The road was almost empty; only a sleepy food seller sat waiting for a final customer. We slowed to a trot, walking swiftly, but not too fast, to avoid attracting attention and gradually I caught my breath. I took Bisi's hand firmly in mine and I could see my fear reflected in her eyes.

Further on, the woman was still busy stirring akara in hot oil and the men at the kiosk were drinking their beer and smoking weed and the music was still blurting unsteadily out of the old radio. I was getting more nervous by the minute. As we passed, one of them turned and stared us down with lusty red eyes.

'Hey, fine girls, come and join us,' he called. The man beside him winked and I shook my head, stumbling after Bisi who was tugging my arm.

'Don't look at anybody,' she hissed.

As we hovered uncertainly at the next junction, three men were running in our direction. One of them was wearing the red baseball cap the wrong way round and another was the man in the white kaftan. They were speaking in low voices, their foreheads glistening with sweat.

As they passed, they didn't even spare us a glance, but as I was about to celebrate that Lanre had escaped, I realised what one of them had been holding.

'Oh no, Bisi! He had the—'

'—torchlight!' Bisi finished.

We began to run down the road the way they had come. I could hardly think as I scanned the slimy gutter, hoping not to find Lanre lying there.

'Oh, Lord, please,' Bisi mumbled and my heart galloped along.

'Hey, ladies, why in such a hurry?' A slim shadow squeezed in between us and we yelped in terror.

Lanre snorted.

'How … what the hell—' I began, and we all burst out laughing in relief.

'How did you escape that situation?' Bisi asked when we calmed down.

'I dropped the torchlight in the middle of the road and sped off. They had no chance. I am not the fastest runner in our school for nothing.'

'Goodness, you had me so worried,' I said.

'Nice to know you care,' he said with a mischievous grin.

I punched him in the arm. 'Of course, I worried! Three angry men chasing you and shouting; "Thief!" I wouldn't have forgiven myself if they hurt you.'

'How do we get back now?' Bisi asked.

'On foot. We're almost there anyway. No point looking for a taxi,' Lanre said.

We walked briskly, no one saying anything. Like a robot I followed Lanre and Bisi through empty streets, placing one foot in front of the other as I held on to the fence, balancing along the river. Now I had time to think, my mind was ablaze with all that had happened. I didn't even notice when we reached the point at the fence where we could climb over.

'Are you all right?' Lanre asked me softly, helping me. I nodded.

'Did you get some answers?' he asked, still holding my hand.

I shrugged. 'Not too sure.'

But his eyes were relentless.

'I'm glad we went. Something happened up there. I just need to … to think it through.'

'I'll go ahead and make sure the way is clear,' Bisi whispered. Her light steps disappeared through the bushes.

'Hey,' Lanre said, pulling me into his arms. 'Tell me if I can do anything,' he murmured.

'You were wonderful today already. You risked your life!' I grinned.

He shrugged. 'I'm glad I could help.' His eyes gleamed in the moonlight and he looked so beautiful I wished he would kiss me.

He was staring at my lips and then leaning in, his scent cloaking me. A shaky breath escaped my throat and his lips were on mine – soft and gentle and probing. My hands moved to his shoulders and the back of his neck to steady myself against the rush of feelings taking over every single nerve in my body.

'I've wanted to do that since I met you,' he said in a low voice.

I wanted to whisper back, but no sound came. I moved in closer to taste more of him. Lanre drew his breath in surprise, then kissed me again, this time deeper, his hands warm and firm on my waist.

'Ehm,' Bisi coughed. 'I hope I'm not spoiling the show, but we really shouldn't push our luck.'

I jerked out of Lanre's hold, Bisi's voice bringing me to my senses.

'Goodnight,' he said, holding on to my hand a moment longer. 'And don't worry too much. I'm sure everything will solve itself.'

Lanre disappeared into the shadows and Bisi and I slipped towards our dorm. We edged the field quietly, staying close to the bushes.

'Lovers' window did its duty again,' Bisi said.

'Heh?'

'That's the name of our bathroom window!' Bisi giggled.

Bisi bobbed her eyebrows and I felt my heart sing.

'So you like him, huh?' she asked.

When I didn't reply she poked me with her finger and I giggled.

'Well, he is definitely cute,' I whispered, hoping the shadows were hiding my wide grin.

'He's a really nice guy. Don't ever tell him I said so, but he is the big brother I never had.'

I smiled.

'Oya, suck in your belly, girl.' She grabbed the two bars around the gap in the window. 'Let's face this last ordeal!'

She struggled and twisted. 'Next time we plan something like this, remind me to skip dinner.'

'I don't think your belly is the issue here,' I whispered, pushing her bum through the bars.

Bisi tumbled inside, snorting softly with laughter. 'You are not trying to say anything against my bum, are you? Because if you are, I'll leave you right there and go to bed.'

I giggled, tugging and twisting. 'No, I'm just putting things in perspective. Don't blame the belly for what the ass is messing up!'

Now she giggled loudly and I fell to the ground.

We had made it. I could feel the weight lifting off us.

Sneaking out of the bathroom, we crept through the corridor and were about to grasp the door handle of Funmi 14 when it opened. Someone was stood in the doorway. They clicked on a torch and shone it in our faces.

'Gone looking for your abiku friend? Sleepwalking again?' Lola sneered. Even in a sleepy voice she sounded mean.

'Mind your business,' Bisi hissed.

'It is my business if I sleep in the same room with a crazy abiku. She better get her act together or I'll report her to Mrs Abimbola.'

'What is there to report?' I cut in.

'Disturbance of the night peace, practising of evil juju, calling on spirits.'

'What?' I cried.

'Are you mad?' Bisi hissed.

'Shh! Quiet!' someone called from inside.

'Considering the history of this place, if Mrs Abimbola so much as hears the word "spirits", you'll be in for your worst nightmare yet!'

'Well done, Lola, only someone as heartless as you would make jokes about Tara having nightmares.'

'You know what, Bisi, in this bloody place, I am proud to be heartless!' Lola snarled. Her eyes gleamed with tears and I was shaken by the force of her words. What was wrong with her?

Lola glanced at me, made the sign of the cross and marched towards the bathroom.

I fell into bed with shaky legs.

'Don't mind that forever-bitch,' Bisi whispered from the bunk above mine. Her voice seemed far away.

The excitement of Lanre's kiss and my relief at being back felt distant now.

I thought I would get answers from visiting the rock, but I was still consumed by never-ending questions. What did Lola mean by 'the history of this place'? Why were people always hinting at Olumo Haven being odd? The word *abiku* seared into me and I felt weak.

As I sank into an uneasy sleep, the priestess's warning took over my thoughts: *Half of you is empty. There is darkness in the emptiness ... if you do not succumb, then the line of cursed souls will grow longer.*

25

Uneasy breathing escaped the girl's lips on the mud bed. The smell of stale sweat and bitter herbs filled the air. An oil lamp flickered feeble light into the room. Outside, owls called, monkeys shrieked and a bush baby whimpered its terrible cry, luring those gullible enough to fall into its trap. The night was thick with fog, heavy with the whispering chants of faraway winds. It was the kind of darkness into which no one would set foot – or they would surely meet a spirit or some fearful creature of the night.

A gust of wind gripped the tattered cloth that covered the door, flinging it aside. An old woman approached and glanced around uneasily, retying her wrapper more tightly against what lay ahead.

Behind her, Olumo Rock loomed like a giant. The old woman was muttering unhappily and when she stepped inside, began stroking the protective charms hanging on a leather band at her neck. She drew a long breath as she took in the scene before her.

The oil lamp cast the shadow of the girl across the mud walls like a long-limbed spirit. Mouth open in a distorted grimace, braids scattered and the huge mound that was her belly, disfiguring her slender body. She wore only a cloth tied round her middle. A chain hung at her throat with two round copper pendants, one larger than the other, and the light conjured strange images from its symbols. The girl watched the woman with dark, cat-like eyes, as if daring her to come closer.

Her head tilted upwards, revealing beautiful high cheekbones, accentuated by delicate tribal marks tattooed on her cheeks. The old woman approached with a nervous hiss and laid experienced hands on the taut belly, feeling with her fingertips.

'Ibeji,' she said, looking up with alarm. 'There are two!'

The girl nodded grimly between gasps, surprising the old midwife.

She shook her head in pity. The girl was too young, sixteen at most. There was no mother to hold her shoulders or murmur words of encouragement, no friend to grip her hand, no husband waiting outside to hear the good news.

The girl cried out, doubling forward and holding her belly, eyes wide with pain and pride.

'It is time,' the midwife muttered. She washed her hands with water from a clay pot, then kneeled in front of the girl's legs to receive the first of the babies into her hands.

'Oya, push,' she hissed. 'It is not a good night for any child to be born, let alone two.'

When the first baby slipped out, she examined it. The child had healthy-looking brown skin and a large amount of shiny, charcoal-black hair. It was a girl with perfectly carved features. A beautiful child. She held up the baby by the leg and slapped her little back until she coughed and gave a shrill cry, high-pitched and angry, as if furious at being so rudely woken. The woman placed the baby in the mother's arms. The girl seemed almost unconscious, but she held the screaming baby firmly.

'Oya, push! The other one is following fast,' the old woman hissed.

The second baby showed an equally generous amount of sleek, charcoal-black curly hair before showing its face.

The old woman gasped as it fell into her hands – another girl, with pale white skin. The midwife's eyes widened in terror.

'What is the meaning of this?'

Beads of sweat rolled down her face as she chanted incantations to the gods for protection. Then she quickly dropped the second twin into the mother's arms and with trembling fingers began searching within the folds of her wrapper.

She pulled out a knife, grasped it firmly and held it aloft: the light of the lamp reflected on the sharp blade as she took a deep breath.

But as she bent to look for the cords connecting the twins to their mother, nourishing them for nine months, she found only one.

'Ahn, ahn...' she muttered, confused.

It was then she saw the full extent of the abomination. The twins were joined to their mother and to each other by a Y-shaped cord. Only one cord for two children!

The knife clattered to the floor, forgotten. The old woman shrieked as she fell backwards in her haste to escape. In that moment, the twins, one black and one white, opened their eyes in a slow parallel motion. Two pairs of piercing green eyes, like drops of dew on elephant grass, stared at the woman.

Olumo echoed her cries up to the sky as she fled to the village, and the young girl rocked the babies, humming quietly.

26

When I opened my eyes, the humming of the girl rang in my head like a chant. There was another sound too. Loud and aggressive, sawing at my nerves. The morning bell. I covered my head with a pillow, but images of the dream flooded back. I saw every detail of the ramshackle hut, the girl groaning in pain and the smell of birth and sweat.

I got out of bed and began straightening the sheets. Who'd have thought I'd become an expert at smoothing bed edges even in the darkness? As I tucked in the bedclothes, my finger slipped too deep, brushing something sharp. I raised the mattress, feeling around until I found it.

A chain with a pendant. The dream rushed back to me and I saw again the chain at the girl's throat. It reminded me of something I'd forgotten and I went to my locker, fumbling feverishly until I felt it in my PU.

I let out a sigh of relief – there it was. A round object, cool beneath my palm. The pendant I had found at the bottom of the little rock after my fall.

I hurried to the bathroom along the quiet corridor, grateful to be alone. Even before switching on the bathroom lights I knew what I would see. In one hand I held the chain I'd seen in my dream, but it had only one pendant. At the bottom of the pendant, I noticed the broken clasp where the smaller one had been.

I opened my other hand, holding the little pendant I had found at Bisi's secret spot.

It was a perfect match.

My hand began to tremble so hard the chain slipped. With a quick motion that surprised me, I snatched up the falling chain and caught it.

Hooking on the broken pendant and slipping the chain around my neck, a sense of calm rushed through me. I leaned back against the bathroom wall and let out a deep sigh of peace.

'Hey, what's up with you today?'

I started out of my thoughts and Bisi threw me a worried look from her desk. 'Are you all right?' she whispered.

I nodded and yawned. 'It was an awful night.'

'The dreams again?'

I nodded, making sure no one was listening, but everyone was busy chatting in the brief minutes before class.

'Well, after all the excitement yesterday, it's no surprise. I also had bad dreams,' Bisi said in a low voice.

I smiled weakly. Nice of her to help me feel less of a weirdo.

'The dreams don't make any sense,' I whispered. 'But they are always so clear, like I am part of them.'

I fiddled with the chain hidden beneath my uniform, rubbing my finger up and down the bulge it made under my blouse.

'Who had my bunk last year?'

'Your bunk?'

'Yes, before I came.'

'It was empty when I arrived and before that I wouldn't know. I only started here last year. How come?'

'Oh, nothing, just wondering.'

I felt Bisi's eyes on me. 'You haven't said if you felt or saw anything yesterday at the rock. You were so weird up there. I was worried.'

'I...' I remembered the sensations that had overpowered me – of feeling heavier, as if I had been wading through thick air. Not being myself.

Bisi squeezed my hand in warning and I saw Mr Bolaji had walked in.

'Eka aro,' we greeted.

He nodded and walked briskly to the blackboard. 'Odún ìbílèè kan tí mo wò rí,' he said and proceeded to write the words in Yoruba.

I stared at the blackboard and swallowed hard.

'Festivals that I have seen in my village,' I read and gasped. Why did I know what the words meant when I didn't understand Yoruba? I couldn't say where one word began or another ended, but I clearly understood what he was saying. I gripped the sides of my desk.

'Festivals in your village,' Bisi whispered.

I stared at her, not able to react.

'Don't worry, he's not going to expect you to write a whole essay on that.'

Mr Bolaji, who had been at the board, turned.

'Who is disturbing my class?' he asked in Yoruba.

'It is the translator giving special services to our oyinbo.' Lola's beloved voice resounded gaily through the room. I didn't care because I had understood Mr Bolaji again! What the hell was going on? I felt queasy and my head began to throb. I jerked up, knocking my pencil off the table, and ran out of the class.

'Did someone just run out?' I heard Mr Bolaji ask.

'It was Tara,' Bisi said. 'She's … ehm … ill. Can I see to her?'

Not waiting to hear any more, I ran for the bathroom and threw up my breakfast of bread and sardine stew.

My body was a painful, heaving mess.

Bisi was leaning against the mirror by the sinks and turned on the tap for me. I washed my face and rinsed my mouth.

She was watching, a worried expression on her face.

I stared at myself in the mirror.

'I think I really am an abiku,' I whispered.

'Oh, no, not that again, Tara, don't be silly!'

'Bisi, I just understood everything Mr Bolaji said in Yoruba! *Before* you translated it!'

'What, like, for real?'

I nodded vigorously.

'Well, that could have been a coincidence.'

'And I understood what Lola said.'

'Anyone could have guessed what Lola said.'

I shook my head. 'Say something,' I said, nervously crossing my arms.

'What?'

'Just say something in Yoruba. Anything!'

Bisi looked at me and I could see she was nervous as well.

'Ṣe o le sọ fun mi nipa rè.'

Like in the classroom, the meaning came to me. I didn't recognise every word, but somehow, I just knew what it meant.

'Can you tell me more about yourself,' I translated.

Bisi raised an eyebrow. 'Èdè t'ole ni.'

'It's a hard language.'

Bisi went pale. 'Okay, this is becoming a tiny bit creepy.' She held up her hands at my worried face. 'There is probably a logical explanation. Maybe your biological mum spoke Yoruba to you when you were little?'

'I was two when I was adopted,' I snapped.

'Oh.'

'And besides she was British. I doubt she could speak a word of Yoruba.'

Bisi tried to say something more, but I shook my head. 'I am an abiku! Why else would I understand Yoruba? I am some kind of old mythical spirit.' I held my belly which was hurting again.

'Or maybe you have a special talent for learning languages?'

'In England my worst grades were in French and German.'

'Maybe it's a talent that shows itself later in life?'

I gave her a look.

'You haven't said what happened last night. Did you discover anything that could make sense of all this?'

I thought of the priestess' words and a chill went through me: *If you do not succumb, then the line of cursed souls will grow longer.*

I shivered. 'I met the old priestess of the rock.'

Bisi raised an eyebrow in surprise.

'She knew things about me … like a diviner or a psychic or something'

Bisi nodded. 'She is a powerful priestess. People go to her for divina—'

'What is it?' I asked.

Bisi was staring at me with wide, alarmed eyes.

'Are you sure it was her? How did you speak to her? How did you understand?'

'Why, what do you mean?'

Bisi spoke quietly, 'I saw her on TV once. She doesn't speak English.'

The tap was leaking, a constant, nerve-racking *drip-drip* sound. I twisted it tight, but the silence engulfing us as we stared at each other was worse.

27

The computer in the library was excruciatingly slow. My fingers twitched. I could have smashed my fist into the screen. I tapped the *Enter* button impatiently, rolling the mouse with trembling hands to click on the results. Bisi sat beside me, not saying anything. She hadn't said much over lunch and neither had I. I was glad she'd come, though I worried I might soon lose her if she followed me on this journey.

An evil spirit that deliberately plagues a family with misfortune. Literal translation of abiku: 'predestined to die'. The abiku deliberately die young. They usually do not live past the age of puberty, then come back to the family, repeating the cycle and causing grief.

I shook my head in panic. No, I wouldn't do that! I loved my parents! I wouldn't want to cause them pain.

But how could I be sure? Was I not a stranger to my own self? Every time I reached inside me, trying to understand, the tips of my fingers grazed a dark, terrifying void.

The priestess's words came back to me. *There is darkness in the emptiness.* I shivered.

The words blurred in front of my eyes. *Born to die, evil spirit, child drawn to the spirit world.*

I got up abruptly, my chair slamming into the table behind me. I couldn't take it any more.

—

'Maxine says hi,' Mum said cheerfully. 'We saw her the other day. She's dyed her hair. It's bright red now.'

'Oh … wow.' I sounded like a Coke gone flat.

I forced myself to act normal. 'Tell her I said hi too.'

Talking to them was tiring. Everything was beginning to feel exhausting.

Dad and Mum seemed more relaxed than last time. Even though it wasn't a video call, I could sense it. There was a brief stretch of silence. I watched the clock on the wall.

'And Dad has some great news,' Mum said.

'Oh, well, I won a big project,' Dad said.

'That's wonderful, Dad, yes, that's … great!'

'Thanks!'

Another pause. 'So, what about you, love? How have you been?'

'Oh, things have been okay, I mean, great. Everything is fine.'

They didn't reply; they were waiting for more. I had to try harder.

'It's cool here. I'm learning Yoruba. I'm getting pretty good at it.'

'That's incredible,' Mum said. 'How's the food? Your dad said it was all too spicy for him.'

'Oh, the food is fine. I've loved almost everything so far, even the leafy stews. The only thing I didn't like was this murky, sour-corn porridge that was so awful, I couldn't even try to pretend to eat it.'

Mum and Dad laughed.

'Are the other kids nice to you?' Mum sounded anxious.

I thought of Lola last night. 'Yes, everyone's so nice and I have two good friends already.'

'Oh, that is wonderful, Tara,' Mum said. 'I am so relieved this is turning out well for you. I have been so worried.' Mum's voice broke.

Abikus deliberately cause grief to their families.

Is that what I was doing?

Abiku children were often ill, fell into trances, had visions.

'Mum, Dad, was I ill much when I was little? Did I have nightmares?'

'Ehm ... no, you were hardly ever ill. The nightmares started recently, as far as we know. If you can't remember having nightmares as a kid, then you probably didn't,' Mum said. 'Is anything bothering you?'

I swallowed the lump in my throat. 'I mean, I... no, I was just wondering, that's all.'

'Have the nightmares not got better?' Dad asked.

'Oh, yes, they have. Everything is fine.' I had to be more convincing. Having them come get me was the last thing I wanted.

'Is everything really okay over there?'

Nothing was okay. I was suffocating, drowning in hopelessness.

'I have to go. We're only allowed ten minutes, so everyone can get their turn.'

'Oh, hon,' Mum seemed like she might cry.

I leaped off the sofa and walked to the window, twirling the pendant between my fingers. My lungs didn't have enough air. I needed to get out of here.

'You make us immensely proud, Tara,' Dad called into the phone. His voice was far away.

'Yes,' Mum added. 'I mean, look at you: all alone in Africa and so grown up about everything.'

I rolled my eyes.

'I'm not all alone in Africa,' I snapped. Why was I feeling so *angry*?

There was a knock at the door and it swung open to reveal a queue forming in the corridor.

I narrowed my eyes, giving the girl at the front a dirty look.

'I'm in a boarding school in Nigeria with hundreds of other girls and we never have a single minute to ourselves.'

Mum and Dad chuckled. 'Ha! That's boarding school for you,' Dad said.

'Bye,' I called, pushing past the girls and out.

Bisi was alone in Funmi 14, ironing on the top of her bunk. She hadn't joined the queue to call home.

'You know, I don't mind you using my bed. Ironing would be much easier down here.'

She shrugged.

'Where is everyone?'

She shrugged again. 'It's Saturday. Everyone is chilling in some corner, I guess. Or in the phone queue.'

'Feel like doing something?'

'Yeah,' Bisi said. 'I'm tired of moping.' She pulled the cable from the socket.

Then we heard shouts and giggles and racing steps.

'Perfect!' Bisi said. 'There is our distraction!' She dragged me down the corridor towards the noise in Funmi 18. I wasn't sure this was what I had wanted, but I let her pull me along. The room was so full we hardly squeezed in. Some illegal source of music was playing hot afro beats. Girls sat huddled together like chickens on poles on the top bunks. More girls crowded the lower beds. The middle of the room was taken up by a serious dancing competition. Two girls were twisting their waists and shaking their bums. Shortly after, they left the circle, followed by hoots and whistles. Two new girls went in and started their own explosive dance, spurred on by another round of screaming. The room was hot with excitement and vibrated with the bass. I let myself get carried away, watching and cheering with the rest. The girls were amazing. Whoever felt like it went into the middle and some got pushed in and had to improvise.

'Go, Tola!' Bisi called. Chidinma went into the circle next. She began a slow move that didn't even go with the beat, but it was so hot and so deadly, her hands caressing her entire body, that it made all the girls giggle hysterically, some falling back on to the beds. When she finished, her eye caught mine and she grinned. ''Tara, Bisi, oya oh! Your turn.'

'Abeg, I no fit dance jareh,' Bisi called with a laugh, shaking her head.

'You think that yellow pawpaw from London can even move her stick waist?'

I jolted in anger at Lola's voice from somewhere above.

'Shut your gutter mouth, Lola,' Bisi snapped.

'Ahn, ahn, Lola, why do you always have to bring your beef?' Chidinma called.

Bisi grabbed my arm. 'Let's get out of here,' she hissed.

But a hot feeling came over me. Fuelled by the atmosphere and seething at Lola, I pulled Bisi back and all the way into the centre. The crowd parted with a cheer. I placed my hands on my waist, looked up at Lola and eyed her, the way I had learned from Bisi, up and down, scoping her disapprovingly. Then I hissed, allowing the sound to sizzle out between my pouted lips as I had often seen the girls do. The crowd went wild and the whooping charged my battery to bursting point. I was on fire and the dance floor was waiting for me to spread my flames.

I began to dance.

My limbs tingled with energy and anger and I allowed them to take over. I twirled my bum, flinging my head and arms this way and that, until I was out of breath. And all the while I scowled with concentration, my teeth biting my bottom lip, my neck bent back so I could watch my bum twerk.

Bisi, who had been standing stiffly beside me, stared. The girls in the room started another round of chanting: 'Go, Tara, go, Tara, go, Tara.' Bisi's open mouth grew into a grin. Before I left the circle, I turned briefly to Lola with a sneer. But to my surprise she didn't scowl back. Instead, a look of shock spread across her face and she was focused on my neck.

'You showed her! You showed her! Na you hot pass!' Bisi gave me a high-five.

I laughed, but as we left the room I touched my neck and realised what Lola had been staring at. My wild dancing had dislodged the chain. It was in plain view and Lola had recognised it.

28

'Where the hell did you get that chain?'

Lola slammed me into the bathroom wall. I was so stunned I could only lean limply and stare.

She began to claw at my collar and I slapped her hand away with such force I jumped at the sound. Lola stepped back, holding her red-raw hand with the other, eyes burning with rage.

'I do not know what you are talking about.' My voice was cold and odd to my ears.

'I saw it while you were prancing around. You cannot deny it,' she hissed. 'Give it to me!'

'The hell...' I stepped forward, fist clenched, then stopped myself. What was wrong with me? I glanced at Lola. What did she know about the chain? Why did it bother her so much that I had it? Was it hers?

My heart cramped at the thought. There was no way I was giving it to her.

'Whose is it?' I asked.

Lola tightened her lips and regarded me silently for a few seconds. Then her scowl loosened and she took a deep breath.

'Omi's!'

'Who is Omi?'

'She used to have your bunk.'

'She has left school?'

'Yes.'

'And?'

'And nothing!'

'So why do you have a problem with me wearing it?'

'I don't… It's just not yours!'

'Well, it's not yours either.' I made to leave the bathroom. 'Where is she now? I could contact her. If she wants it back, I could…'

But I couldn't get the last word past my lips.

Lola shook her head angrily as the door swung open and two girls walked in. She jumped, seeming embarrassed, as if caught doing something forbidden and quickly left.

In the bathroom mirror my face looked flushed and I didn't recognise myself. I stroked the chain hidden beneath my dress, then turned on the tap, splashing cold water on my warm cheeks.

'Hey, I loved your moves today, girl!' Chidinma grinned as she washed her hands.

I smiled. 'Thanks. I didn't even know I had any moves. Your dancing inspired me.'

She laughed.

'Chidinma, do you know who had my bunk before I came?'

'Oh, that was Omi.'

'And what was she like? No one's mentioned her before.'

'She was a bit of a weirdo. Never spoke to anyone, always moping around. I don't think she had a single friend. Why are you asking?'

'Oh, you know … just interested. Why did she leave?'

'Hmm, I don't know. Come to think of it, no one really knows. It was sudden. From one day to the next she packed her things and was gone. Mrs Abimbola announced she had been called back home, but we snatched up some gossip that she was expelled for bad conduct.'

'Oh, that's strange, isn't it?' I said, my hand at my neckline.

'What do you mean?'

'Well, that no one knows the reason. That she didn't have any friends.'

'Yes, but she was the quiet type. Kept to herself, disappearing often. You hardly noticed her when she was present and then, hours later, you'd realise she'd been long gone. She always seemed out of place. Like she never really fit.'

29

I was loosening my plaits when I heard it the first time. In that same moment, there was a power failure, and everyone in Funmi 14 began stumbling about for their torches, so I thought I'd imagined it. The ceiling fan squeaked to a halt and sweat instantly seeped out of my pores. It was the second power failure that day – something I still hadn't got used to. I sighed, snatching up a book to cool myself.

Then it came again – a low, long moan that went right through my gut. I sat upright but no one else seemed to have noticed. Rosemary had set up a gas lamp and was helping Lola loosen her corn rows. She continued her incessant chattering as if nothing had happened. Bisi hadn't yet returned from the bathroom and Chidinma and Halima were already curled up in their bunks, sleeping.

I glanced at Lola. She was cleaning nail polish from

her toes, lost in thought. She'd been giving me strange looks all evening and I felt more uncomfortable than ever in her presence.

I walked to the window, peering through the mosquito netting. Nothing. Just dark grey bushes. My hands gripped the bars tightly and I shivered. Did we actually climb through the bathroom window and creep through the night to Olumo Rock? The idea seemed absurd and distant, like a hazy memory. These past weeks, my thoughts had begun to jumble. I struggled to distinguish between reality and my dreams. I was constantly tired from the exhausting nights. The nightmares stole my sleep and squeezed their way into my days.

The ten o'clock gong sounded and I pulled away from the window. Lights out.

Rosemary switched off the gas lamp and Lola climbed into bed.

Bisi slipped in, muttering. 'Of course I forgot my torch and had to shower in complete darkness. Goodnight, everyone.'

'Goodnight,' I replied, as she climbed into her bunk.

Rosemary and Lola were still whispering and giggling as they often did after lights out, when I heard it again. A long, hair-raising wail ripped through the air. I gripped my bedclothes and Bisi's bunk creaked above me.

'What the hell was that?'

'I heard it before but thought I imagined it,' I said.

There was a snort from Lola's bed. 'We are in boarding school,' she said. 'It is normal to hear strange noises at night. Rosemary, did you hear anything?'

'No,' Rosemary replied. 'What did you guys hear?'

'It was like a sad wail or something,' Bisi said.

'Maybe our Olumo Haven spirit is back. It's been a while,' Lola sniggered.

'Ah, no! Please don't say so,' Rosemary said.

'Or maybe this time it's Lady KoiKoi. I am surprised she hasn't visited us yet.'

'Who is Lady KoiKoi?' I asked, immediately regretting my question.

'Who wants to explain to London?' Lola sneered.

Bisi sighed. 'It's a stupid story about a ghostly woman who runs around wearing a single red-heeled shoe. She is searching for her other one, so you only hear the sound of one heel – *koi, koi, koi*.'

'But what does she have to do with boarding school?'

'The tale is that she used to be a teacher, an elegant and beautiful teacher, but a wicked one. She would flog students for the fun of it. So one night she was cornered by them...'

'And then?' I whispered.

'They flogged her to death,' Lola finished. 'And when they found her, she was only recognisable by her one red shoe. Now she forever haunts boarding schools, searching the corridors for her lost shoe … *koi* … *koi* … *koi.*'

There was a brief gloomy silence. Halima switched on her torch light. 'What's going on?' she asked sleepily.

'Ghost-story time,' Lola replied.

'How about the one with the girl at boarding school who takes off her head at night and places it in her lap to weave her hair?' Rosemary whispered.

'That's another good one,' Lola said, and in the half-darkness I could see her mischievous grin. 'Wouldn't it be so much easier if we could take off our heads to weave our hair? No need to stretch your hands up for hours.' She sat in her bunk, her bedsheet pulled up to hide her head. Then she squeezed her pillow into a tight ball on her lap and pretended to plait hair on the pillow. She looked absolutely ghostly in the dimly lit room. Halima giggled nervously, but was silenced by the long, sad moan from outside. Only its whispery ends reached us through the window.

'Oh, no! It really is the Haven ghost,' Rosemary cried. 'It's back!'

'What do you mean, back?' I asked.

'Last year we heard this noise almost every night,' Halima said. She sounded close to tears.

A hiss came from Lola's bunk. 'And now everyone will go haywire again. Mrs Abimbola will begin extra prayers against evil spirits and juniors will call their parents to come pick them up.' Lola yawned loud.

'Well, it did sound creepy. What in the world was it?' Bisi asked quietly.

'Someone close the window,' Halima hissed.

'Close it yourself, you're right beside it,' Lola snapped.

'Chidinma is closer,' Halima said in a whiny voice.

'Chidinma is sleeping,' Rosemary replied.

'Chidinma!' Halima called. 'Close the window!'

No answer.

Suddenly a loud, horrible wail erupted from Lola's bed.

Screams and yelps came from all sides.

Lola giggled hysterically.

'You guys are so silly,' Bisi said. She stomped down the ladder and closed the window. The others laughed, but I couldn't. I was lying very still, the awful wail resonating in my ears.

30

The drums were loud, but it was the shrill, rhythmic, metallic gong that was deafening. People gathered around a hollow cave. A huge slab of stone loomed over the crowd.

A young woman kneeled on the ground, hands tied in front of her with shreds of cloth. Her feet were bound together so tight that the skin at her ankles was bruised a dark purple. She wore a loose indigo tunic and a chain with two pendants dangling at her neck. A man with a sharp cap and a bushy beard stood before her. Wide trousers were secured at his waist with string and his upper body was bare. Sweat glistened on his chest and belly. He was wielding a knife and with each movement of his arm, displayed bulging muscles. The woman was terrified, her eyes red and swollen. Sweat dripped down her face, trickling between the two traditional marks tattooed on her cheeks. She kept shaking her head, but no words came from her lips.

The drumming and the gong ceased as a group of women appeared on the path. They were singing and clapping, leading two girls of about twelve years old, dressed in white cloth. Their skin was painted from head to toe with chalky white dots. They had long, curly hair the colour of deep night. It glowed in the bright sunlight, falling over their shoulders like lazy coiled snakes. But this was not the most striking thing about them. Their faces were the same, but like night and day – one of them very pale, the other a deep brown. Out of those identical faces stared eyes, greener than sharply carved gem stones, glittering in the hot afternoon sun.

They held their heads high, eyes aiming straight ahead.

The women's song was accompanied by the *seke-seke* sound of the panseke trees which trembled without a gust of wind. The women brought the girls forward and silently moved to join the crowd. Waiting.

The kneeling woman tried to touch the twins and the man pulled her hands away roughly when an old woman appeared at the mouth of the cave. She was so shrivelled and bent by age that she did not need to stoop under the rock. Her hair was white as snow, her hands covered by thick veins crisscrossing her skin that was as brittle as grass in dry season. She looked down, her gaze wandering across the crowd, before landing on the twins.

The man with the knife began to speak, but the old woman raised a hand to stop him. The man went quiet and the crowd hushed.

The woman stooped lower, painfully, and one could almost hear her bones creak. She drew a circle on the ground with a piece of chalk, then another that intersected the first.

She stretched out a claw-like hand and called:

'Bring me their hair!'

'No! Don't touch them!' the mother cried, but the man pushed her away. Her face slammed the floor, bone hitting rock.

The children cried out as the man approached, slipping shaking hands into each other's.

'Cut off the hair, cut off the hair,' the women chanted. The drums and the shrill metallic gong beat wildly.

The man grabbed the twins' hair, entwining it and winding it around his arm. Then he raised his knife and a moment later, held up the curls like a trophy of wriggling snakes.

The old priestess indicated for him to drop the bundle into the circles she had drawn.

She groaned softly as she sat on the ground. Her fingers hovered over the hair, her eyes upturned so only the whites were visible. She swayed and trembled, murmuring incoherently.

The twins cowered like bedraggled shorn sheep ready for slaughter. Their mother lay at their feet in a puddle of blood, but she was no longer crying. She struggled up, cursing, her eyes fixed on the circles and her body swaying like she was in a trance. The chanting heightened and the voice of the priestess rose almost to a scream, then her eyes cleared and she pointed to the twins. 'Kill them!'

The drumming went wild as the man turned to the twins, his taut muscles flexing as he brandished the knife. The mother's body convulsed and her face took on a look of such pure hatred that people gasped. Her pupils were stone-black.

The man grabbed one of the twins by the short stubble of her hair, pulling her head back to expose her throat. As he raised the knife, a snarl tore through the air. A leopard appeared on the rock, landing elegantly on silent paws. It raised its head and growled, a deep rumbling sound. Then it set back on its hind legs and stretched its front paws, ready to spring in attack, honing in on the bearded man through animal-green, slanted eyes. By the time it landed on the man's chest, he had dropped the knife, and let go of the child with a grunt of surprise.

People screamed, stumbling over each other and running in all directions.

The old priestess retreated into the cave like a shadow, fear in her eyes. The mother and the twins were nowhere to be seen. All that remained were the two ropes with which her hands and feet had been tied and a heap of deep black hair.

31

I woke, dazed, feeling like I had spent the night in another world. Another time. A memory of green eyes, thick black coils of snakes and dotted fur made me tremble.

I planted my feet on the ground, trying to connect myself back into reality when a scream cut through the Sunday morning air. The scream stopped briefly, then continued in the same panicked high pitch. Heads began to pop up from the covers in the bunks around me. Outside in the corridor, a shuffling of feet and muffled voices made me nervous.

'What is happening?' Halima croaked in a sleepy voice. But everyone was already hurrying through the door.

The screaming was coming from Funmi 5.

'My hair! My hair!' someone wailed as I tried to weave through the crowd of drowsy-looking girls in nightwear.

'What is this racket?' Mrs Abimbola's voice cut through the hubbub. 'Children, it is too early in the morning for this kind of drama!'

She pushed past me and I squeezed in swiftly after her.

A girl was crouched in the middle of the room, holding her head. Her name was Salewa. She was crying, shoulders heaving, and two girls were holding her. I remembered her because she had very long, beautiful hair. Even when plaited, it reached down, shiny and thick, past her shoulders. Someone had once said how Salewa's hair had gone to her head. She didn't need to keep feeling so special because of it.

But now all that was left were scanty strands standing upright on her head.

'For goodness' sake, what happened to you, girl?' Mrs Abimbola asked.

'I don't know,' Salewa wailed, tears and snot dripping down her chin. 'I just woke up like this, and Isi and Tokunbo screamed when they saw me.'

'What devil did this?' Mrs Abimbola asked, looking around the room. 'There are going to be serious consequences!'

'Strange, strange, strange!' Lola's voice came through the door. 'Someone in Funmi 14 was shouting, "Cut off the hair!" all night. We could not sleep. As usual.'

Rosemary appeared in the doorway beside her, nodding in agreement.

My legs went weak.

'What?' Mrs Abimbola called. 'What do you mean, Lola? Speak up, girl!'

'Chidinma woke Rosemary last night and that's when I woke too.' Lola waved a hand at Rosemary.

'Chidinma! Someone get Chidinma here!' Mrs Abimbola called. 'In fact, everybody out, apart from the girls of Funmi 5 and Funmi 14. Everyone else, please go about your business and prepare yourselves for Sunday devotion.'

I glanced at Lola, but she was staring at Salewa, shaking her head sadly.

Chidinma poked her head through the door.

'Yes, Ma,' she mumbled. 'You called me.' Then she saw Salewa and her eyes widened.

'What is this I am hearing about cutting off hair? What did you hear last night?'

Chidinma took a step back. Her eyes darted nervously around the room, then landed on me.

She raised an eyebrow, her face betraying surprise, then fear. She stared at the scanty savannah on Salewa's head. 'Tara was talking in her sleep. She often does that.' She stopped and her eyes caught mine guiltily. I didn't know what to feel or think. I just waited, like all the others, to hear what I had done.

'She was shouting, "Cut off the hair!"'

Chidinma spoke so quietly her voice was a whisper.

'Speak up, girl,' Mrs Abimbola barked impatiently. 'What was she shouting?'

'Cut off the hair.'

'Cut off the hair?' Mrs Abimbola repeated. 'Why would you be shouting that, Tara?'

The scene from my dream flashed through my mind. The drumming, the twins and their mother, the bearded man with the knife and the old woman crying, 'Cut off their hair.'

I shuddered. 'I … I don't know, Ma.'

'What do you mean, you don't know? You should know if you were the one shouting. Why were you shouting that?'

'I guess I was having a … a nightmare.'

'She is always having nightmares,' Lola hissed. 'We have not had one night of peace since she arrived. Always screaming and walking around like an abiku searching for her iyi-uwa or whatever it is they do.'

'The Haven ghost is back, Ma. We heard it last ni—' Rosemary began. Mrs Abimbola silenced her with a cold stare.

The girls of Funmi 5 gasped and began whispering among themselves. Salewa looked at me with red swollen eyes as if I was a demon. As if I was the Haven ghost itself. I longed for the ground to swallow me. Could I have done this?

'Stop spreading your lies, Lola,' Bisi yelled. She burst through the crowded doorway, holding her toothbrush still dripping wet. 'You have been jealous of Tara since she got here. Mrs Abimbola, please don't believe Lola's lies.'

Chidinma shook her head slowly at Bisi.

'It is true. I heard her shouting "cut off the hair" last night. I tried to calm her and called her name a couple of times, but she didn't wake up. She kept on calling "cut off the hair" in this strange voice. Like a...' She stopped, glancing around uneasily. 'So, I just covered my head with my pillow. It was really scary.'

'Tara would never have done this,' Bisi yelled, jerking her finger at Salewa's head. 'Tell them, Tara!'

I felt as if I was in a trance. Like my bones were filled with lead, not marrow. Maybe I *was* an abiku? The wicked spirit in me had taken over, made me have nightmares, made me do things I didn't want.

'I am so sorry,' I said. 'I ... I sleepwalk sometimes ... and ... I don't know what I am doing when I sleepwalk.'

Salewa shrieked and burst into tears.

'What a sick person,' Lola said.

'No.' Bisi shook her head. 'Stop it, Tara.'

Mrs Abimbola who had been listening in silence all this while raised her hands.

My eyes burned and tears dripped down the tip of my nose.

'Where did you put the hair?' Mrs Abimbola asked.

'Let's check her things. Maybe she wants to use the

hair for some evil juju,' someone said. 'We have to get Salewa's hair back before it is too late.'

There was a scramble for the door as the girls rushed out.

Chidinma looked at me, shoulders hanging dejectedly.

Mrs Abimbola gestured. 'Oya, Tara, follow me. We are going to have a serious talk. Salewa, dear, go and shower, afterwards come to my office.'

'We found it, we found Salewa's hair!' Girls' voices screamed excitedly and my heart sank.

'It was in a plastic bag under Tara's bed along with the scissors!'

Bisi squeezed my hand. 'Tara!' she whispered.

I tore my hand out of hers. Her eyes widened with shock. I guess she had seen the capitulation in mine.

The acceptance.

32

U *p ... aim ... swing ... cut ...*
My fingers burned like fire. Every time I raised my arm to swing the machete through the thick grass, I winced. Blisters had long since formed on my palms and they ripped open with each stroke of my trembling hand.

A group of girls passed by, but this time I didn't care. At the beginning, when they first saw me on punishment, I died of shame. Everyone in the Funmi Dorm knew already. But the girls from the other dorms didn't, and so when they came out in the atrium, the whispering and discussions began. I could see their disgust.

Swing up!

I raised my arm, heaving the machete. Then aimed, swinging low to hit the grass close to the roots.

Wince.

Pain.

Swing up!

'Tara.' I heard Bisi through the window behind me. I ignored her and continued. 'Tara,' she called again. 'Are you okay?'

I sighed and stopped briefly. Pain shot through my back muscles. Blood rushed through my veins, out of my head. I swayed.

The sun had burned my face and salty sweat streamed into my eyes.

I turned slowly and nodded. Bisi was holding a glass of water through the bars of a window.

I shook my head vehemently.

'Stop being stubborn,' she hissed. 'Even if you did it, you know deep inside you didn't mean to. If it were true that you are an abiku, which I really do not believe … but if it *were*, then it's just the evil spirits making you do things. It's not *you*. Don't punish yourself more than necessary.'

I shook my head again. 'I deserve all this. I am evil,' I whispered.

Bisi shook her head frantically, and I turned my back on her.

I thought of the nylon bag they'd found under my bed, filled with Salewa's hair. What had I planned to do with it? Mrs Abimbola had asked me the question over and over.

'This will have serious consequences,' she had said. 'I will have to inform your parents.'

I quickly pushed the thought of Dad and Mum away. I didn't have the strength to think of them now. I could not begin to imagine what they would say.

I ignored Bisi's cursing and continued cutting the grass. I had not even cut a tenth of what I was meant to and I must have been out here for two hours already.

Tears mingled with the sweat running down my face.

I sank back into my rhythm, chanting the words under my breath.

Up … aim … swing … cut …

The tray trembled as if there was an earthquake. But it was just my arms, struggling to lift it. My hands were a mess. I had not finished cutting the lawn and tomorrow the ordeal would continue. Mrs Abimbola had allowed me to shower and change for dinner. Not that I was hungry. I felt sick and wanted to curl up in bed. Didn't want to be here in the loud dining hall under the scrutiny of the entire school. Everyone must have heard by now, even the boys. Curious stares followed me.

Bisi was doing a lot of talking, obviously trying to get my mind on to other things. But how? How could I possibly think of anything else?

I was an abiku, possessed, born to die young!

I almost stumbled into Bisi who had stopped at our usual table. My heart jolted when I saw him. Lanre was watching me, a kind, consoling look on his face. I wanted to cry out as desperate feelings hurled through me. What must he think of me?

'Are you okay?' he asked quietly. I nodded, avoiding his gaze. I couldn't stand those earnest, warm eyes on me right now. I shifted my boiled plantains from one side of the plate to the other.

None of us spoke. Hushed whispers came from the other end of the table.

'Mehn, we have an economics test tomorrow and I have not understood anything in my book yet,' Bisi said, and I was happy for the change of topic. Bisi chatted away with Lanre and his friend until the end of the meal.

'Will you come to the wall later?' Lanre asked, as we returned our trays to the shelves in front of the kitchen. I shook my head and turned to go.

'Hey, Tara, please?' he asked. 'Let's talk. I'm here for you, you know.' His hand on my arm felt so good. 'I don't care about all that gossip going on, I just want you to talk to me.'

I shrugged off his hand. 'You should keep away. I am not good for the people around me,' I said, and left him.

33

Everywhere I went, eyes turned from me. A hurt that grazed me again and again until I felt raw. I had become an outcast. After assembly, friends surrounded Salewa, trying to cheer her up. The hateful stares of her friends seared through me, melting any hopes I still had that I might have been dreaming.

Bisi was at my side all the while, even though I'd stopped talking to her. To anybody.

During break time, Lanre walked over holding two cans of Coke. I ignored his smile and when he tried cornering me, I walked away, leaving him there like an idiot.

'Oh, Lanre, you are just the person I've been looking for,' I heard Lola's sickly-sweet voice purr. I couldn't help glancing back. She'd placed a hand on his shoulder and had moved in much too close to whisper in his ear. He was still watching me, hurt in his eyes. He looked at Lola and nodded at what she was saying. Then he laughed and handed her one of the drinks. I felt something deflate in my chest, a sharp pain between my ribs. *It's the best thing. Keep everyone far away before you hurt them. They'll be relieved, even if they don't admit it.*

When Bisi wasn't looking, I escaped back to the dorm after lunch. I breathed in the peaceful emptiness of our room. There were no awkward stares, no sudden quiet when I walked in. I sank into my bed, wanting to bury my face, when I noticed a letter on my pillow. *National Identity Management Commission, Abeokuta*. The call to the commission had made me hopeful, despite all my doubts about Jimi. They'd told me to give them my address, since I was not reachable by phone. Would I finally get an answer to at least one of my hundreds of questions?

The letter almost tore with the envelope in my haste to read it.

Dear Ms Walther,

We regret to inform you that we cannot provide any information on persons named Jimi or Jimmy or to related names Jakob and James due to data protection and privacy laws. If you provide a surname and can prove your relationship as his daughter, then we will be happy to look into the matter. We regret that for now we cannot be of assistance and wish you success in your search.

What had I expected? I already had the answer I needed. I was an abiku, possessed, and that was all there was to know.

The door whirled open.

'Oh, there you are!' Bisi cried, throwing her school bag up on to her bunk.

She glanced at the letter in my hands and sat down beside me.

'Did they write?' She was already reading the letter that hung limply from my hand.

'I'm so sorry,' she said softly.

I shrugged.

'Well, it doesn't mean he isn't here, or that he doesn't exist, you know. He just isn't registered in Abeokuta. Or—'

'Leave it be, Bisi.'

'But—'

'What is it to you?' Why the hell was she trying to find reasons to make me feel better? I did not deserve it.

'Why are you still my friend?' My voice was hoarse and mean. 'Can't you see what a wretched, evil person I am? Why are you wasting your time on me?'

Her eyes were wide and bruised.

'Because I care for you, you are my friend and I would never abandon you. I know deep inside you are good.'

But that was exactly the one thing I did not know. I had absolutely no idea who I was or if there was good inside of me.

The image of Salewa's sad-looking tufts of hair came to my mind.

I couldn't hurt any more people. I couldn't be responsible for another action like that. 'Leave me alone, will you?' I was yelling now. 'Why won't you get it?'

Bisi stared at me in disbelief.

I bit my lip, uncertain if I had gone too far, but it was too late.

She left the room without a word.

34

'How much?' I whispered, checking to see if a teacher was in sight. The little girl selling kola nuts brought the tray down from her head.

'Two hundred naira,' she said, grinning.

The hawkers knew we weren't officially allowed to shop through the gate. But everyone did it. All you needed to do was 'drop something' for the gate man. One of the blisters on my palm popped as I pulled a bundle of money out of my PU pocket. I handed her a crumpled two-hundred naira note.

'Sista, where is my own?' the gate man called, when I was safely back inside. Passing him one of the kola nuts, I slipped the other two into my pocket. I had never tried them before, just heard some girls talk about it. Students chewed kola nuts when they had exams. It was meant to work like coffee and help you concentrate while you studied. I needed it for other reasons. I needed to keep awake through the night.

I chewed every single bulb of the large chestnut-like nuts, allowing the bitterness to seep into my gums and down my throat. I wished the juice would remain bitter, but to my annoyance, sweetness always emerged. My mouth couldn't stand the taste. The taste of anything. It was as if I was drying up inside, becoming hollowed out. Even my saliva felt rationed, my mouth a scorched riverbed, my throat a desert, and my voice a raspy, arid wind.

If they didn't keep me awake all night, maybe they would at least stop me sleeping too deeply. Stop me from dreaming. From doing terrible things.

In the bathroom, I let cold water run into the sink and bathed my blistered hands. It was a distant pain, as if it belonged to someone else. Even my face in the mirror seemed different. I was like an unfeeling ghost. And like a ghost, I followed the girls when it was time to shower, time for dinner or for prep. Once in a while I would think of Bisi or Lanre. Lanre kissing me. Did all that really happen?

Bisi spent every moment in her bed reading.

'Even Bisi has given up on London,' Lola said. No one in the room replied. Bisi didn't bother looking up.

Past midnight, the darkness of the dorm was heavy. Thick clouds hid the moon. The prospect of staring at the bottom of Bisi's bunk one moment longer suffocated me. My senses, which had been dulled and glazed all day, were now alert and bristling. I was wide awake in the middle of the night and there was nothing to do but lie here. I groaned.

The snores and other sleeping sounds of my five roommates were like an orchestra. I kept myself busy. The thick, nasal snore was Chidinma. The raspy breathing was definitely Halima. Unlike her bitchy, aggressive self, Lola was surprisingly peaceful in her sleep.

Suddenly there was a distant moaning. Was it the Haven ghost? I was upright in a second, my head cocked towards the window. There it was again, a long, sad wail. I hesitated, then slipped out of bed, my hot feet enjoying the coolness of the floor beneath them. I grabbed the bars of the window and stared out. Silhouettes of trees and bushes shivered as if jostled by an invisible force.

When the moan came again I felt it rip through me. My blisters burst as I gripped the bars tighter and the agony from my palms blended with the throb of another familiar pain. A desperate longing. Instinctively, I knew where it came from. I thought of the cave underneath Bisi's secret rock. A cold, desperate feeling unfurled inside me, causing my common sense to curl up and retreat. My heart thudded wildly against my ribcage as I willed myself to resist. Why did it feel like the wail was calling me? Was I imagining things, or did it sound like *'Jimi!'*? I covered my ears and flung myself into bed. My pillow was too hot, too heavy. And now I wished I hadn't chewed all that kola nut. I wished for nothing more than to fall sleep and not hear this terrible sound.

35

When I got out of bed next morning, my first thought surprised me like a jack-in-the-box. I wanted Dad and Mum. A wave of homesickness hit me in a rush, I could almost feel their arms around me. Dad, thin and tall, his hair much too long and hanging inside his glasses; Mum, soft and warm. Mrs Abimbola would probably have called them by now to inform them of my crime and punishment. I cringed at them knowing. Were they worried? How on earth would I explain that?

A gust of wind swept through the open window and the curtains billowed.

'Ahn-ahn, what is this?' Lola grumbled, pulling her cover around her shoulders. 'Has Harmattan come or what? Chidinma, abeg close the window jareh, it's cold.'

'My skin feels dry like leather,' Halima muttered, rubbing sleep out of her eyes. 'How come the winds are so early this year? It's just November.'

I blocked out their chatter, consumed by my thoughts. I would call them on Saturday. I'd tell Dad and Mum that I wanted to go home.

Home. A tight lump formed in my throat at the thought. Wasn't that where I was meant to be? This was the only place I felt whole, safe, where I belonged. I had felt lost and rootless before coming here.

Searing pain tore through my temples and I winced. How could I think of leaving?

Rosemary caught my eye as she grabbed her towel, but she quickly looked away and left the room.

I dragged myself up and followed the others to the bathroom.

The fatigue in my body was like I had weights attached to my joints. The two-day punishment and the lack of sleep were getting to me and I was tired beyond words. I caught Bisi watching me from across the room. We used to do everything together, even brush our teeth, and now we were at far ends of the bathroom, not talking. She had a pained expression on her face and when I turned away, her eyes had filled with tears.

A shower door opened and Lola came out. She eyed us with a wicked glint.

'Oh, oh, oh, what a heartbreaking sight,' she said. 'No side by side any more.'

Bisi almost choked on her toothpaste, but only managed to shake her head. Even Bisi was tired of fighting.

Lola just laughed and walked out.

We were hardly dressed when Mrs Abimbola arrived in Funmi 14, her eyes sharp like a hawk. With hands folded behind her back she inspected the beds, made sure lockers were closed and checked our uniform skirts touched our knees. Like a sniffer dog chasing a trail, she searched the room, sure she would find something. Like she could already smell it.

She traced her finger along the top of our lockers and when she held it out covered with red dust, I imagined her tail wagging.

'As you might have noticed, the Harmattan wind has come this morning. From now on, more dusting will take place in the dorm. Cleanliness is next to godliness!'

Lola rolled her eyes and Mrs Abimbola pounced.

'Lola, I don't like that your skirt is always so tight and if I am not mistaken I have told you this before!'

She sat on my bed and glared at Lola.

'Oh, I must have put on weight again,' Lola replied nonchalantly. Halima snorted and began coughing to cover it up. Lola was the skinniest girl in Funmi 14.

'Halima, yours is much too long. Do not feel you are any better than the rest. Religion or not, we have a school uniform, and the correct length is slightly below the knee.'

Bisi raised her eyebrows.

'Lola, last warning if you don't want to smell pepper!'

Lola's face remained indifferent, almost defiant, but Mrs Abimbola did not say anything.

She glanced around the room again, as if she was unhappy nothing worse was amiss. No one even dared breathe. When Mrs Abimbola began her speeches and sermons it was better to be quiet. Every comment or wrong move prolonged the agony.

'There is a reason it is called a uniform. Uniformity means sameness. We are not here to show off our bodies or to make statements. We are here to learn. This is a decent institution.' Her voice grew louder as she saw Lola's unconcern. I rolled my eyes inwardly.

'I will not condone any girls falling off the right track. Not on my watch. I want you all to leave this school in two years' time as respectful, respectable, god-fearing young women. Whichever god that may be,' she added, looking in Halima's direction. 'Have you heard me?' She glanced at her watch and got up. 'I will check the other rooms and walk to the dining room at a reasonable pace. If anybody gets there after me, that person will clean the toilets next week.'

She glanced round at us one last time, then left.

'Goodness, what a bore every morning,' Lola hissed.

I snatched my rucksack out of my locker to check I had the right books when I saw a bunch of keys lying on my bed. Mrs Abimbola's! I snatched them up and was about to run after her when a thought struck me.

She had files on every boarding student. I had seen her pull out my file to make a note the day Lola and I had sat in her office. What if there was a file on Omi? Maybe I could find out what happened – or get an address or telephone number. I could call her and ask where she got the chain.

I slipped the keys into my pocket, almost bumping into Lola. She looked at me with narrowed eyes and I hurried out before she said anything. Bisi was waiting in the corridor, seeming lost. We usually went for breakfast together and she obviously wondered if she should wait for me.

But if I wanted to do this, I had to go right away. Mrs Abimbola could notice her keys were missing any minute. I walked past Bisi without a second glance, heading to the bathrooms. They were empty as I'd hoped.

As soon as the dorm sounded quiet, I slipped out and hurried down the corridor to Mrs Abimbola's office. I fumbled the keys into the lock with trembling fingers, testing each one to see which would fit.

36

A huge wall of files faced me. How on earth would I find the right one? Looking closely, I saw the folders were arranged alphabetically and I realised I didn't even know Omi's surname.

I kneeled in front of 'W' and found Walther. I reached out, tempted, but stopped myself. No time for fooling around.

What was I going to do?

I couldn't open every single file. What if they hadn't kept it? She'd left the school over a year ago.

'Think!' I hissed to myself.

There were only a few folders after mine – one with a label which said: *Miscellaneous*.

I grabbed it and browsed the registers inside. One title read: *Problem Cases*.

Chidinma had said there were 'problems' with Omi. Rumours she'd been expelled.

The first and biggest section was for a student called Omotara Ilori. I stared at the name, irritated. Was Omi the same person as Omotara? I didn't like the way my name was hidden within hers. A part of it.

I traced my finger along the entries and stopped at *Funmi14*.

Omotara *was* Omi.

I slid to the ground, leaning against the back of Mrs Abimbola's brown sofa as I turned the pages feverishly.

I read out loud, trying to make sense of the words.

'One living, distant relative ... poor socio-economic background ... school scholarship ... very good grades ... quiet student.'

My fingers twirled the pendant at my neck as I tried to understand the feelings erupting inside of me. Who was she? Why did she leave the school? Was it a coincidence that she had a name so similar to mine?

I glanced at my watch. Mrs Abimbola would be back at the dining hall now!

The next pages contained documents concerning her scholarship and grades. But at the bottom, close to the end of her file, a last entry stood out.

'Expulsion for indecent conduct ... aggression towards co-student ... name of the other student withheld.'

I slammed the file shut. I hadn't really found out anything.

Disappointed, I shoved the file back. I had to run, right now.

A red notebook that must have slithered out of the file clattered loudly to the ground and I jumped, listening for approaching footsteps. The corridor was silent. I breathed out shakily and turned back to the sketchbook in my hands. Its pages were filled with beautiful portraits. If this was Omi's, she was really good.

I choked as a face stared back at me.

A face out of my dream.

The woman. The mother of the twins.

Mrs Abimbola's frame blocked the entrance of the dining hall like a bouncer. I ran faster, thoughts scrambling for excuses. When I reached her, she stepped into the hall and with a sinking feeling, I realised she wanted to make an example of me.

Everyone went quiet and a sea of faces turned on me.

'Tara Walther, you have overstepped the limit of my patience and sympathy. You will…'

I held out the bunch of keys with a shaking hand.

'I have been searching all over the dorm to give you your keys,' I gasped.

She scanned me warily through two angry slits. 'Where did you find them?'

'On my bed where you sat this morning.'

Reluctantly, her face loosened out of its scowl. 'You are very, very lucky. You were about to see the red part of my eye!'

I scuttled away.

'Discipline!' Mrs Abimbola shouted. 'Discipline is everything!'

But I wasn't listening. My heart was thumping in excitement at the thought of the little sketchbook I had stolen from her office, which lay hidden away beneath my pillow.

37

'Will you stop bitching around, Rosi!' Lola hissed. She was cutting strips of newspaper into a pile.

Rosemary was trying to get at the scissors Lola was holding, but Lola twisted out of reach.

'Give them back jareh, and stop calling me that!' Rosemary looked upset.

'*Rosi, will you dance with me, come now, dance, Rosi?*' Lola began to sing.

'Silence over there!' Mrs Soyemi, the fine arts teacher called from the front.

'What's that song? I think I know it,' Tunde asked.

Lola snorted. 'Ahn-ahn, don't you know Blacky's song from the nineties? He sang it especially for Rosemary here. But she doesn't want to be called "Rosi" in that local kind of way. She wants to be posh.'

Rosemary scowled and made another attempt to get at the scissors, but Lola ignored her and kept on cutting.

'Lola!' she cried angrily.

Mrs Soyemi straightened. 'Lola, what is the problem?'

'Nothing, Ma,' Lola replied, slamming the scissors on Rosemary's desk. 'Rosi is just being childish as usual.'

Some boys behind giggled and Rosemary glared at her artwork, eyes brimming with tears.

Bisi shook her head, then glanced at me with a frown.

I ignored her. My mind was on Omi, or rather Omotara. In my school bag the red sketchbook lay like a bright, blatant incrimination. I still hadn't found a moment to myself to look at it. I yanked my bag up and closed the zip.

'Should we go to the secret place today?' Bisi asked.

I froze.

'We should talk. I've had a weird thought I want to discuss with you.'

I shrugged, then slowly shook my head. That wasn't a good idea. For a brief second, she looked hurt, but she tightened her lips into a straight line, her face unreadable.

I felt like a brute. 'Bisi … I…' But before I could say anything else, Mrs Soyemi was glaring at me over her glasses.

When the bell rang I had hardly progressed with my project.

'So you all know what to do!' Mrs Soyemi called above the racket of students scraping their chairs back.

'You are free to choose the materials as long as they stick to your cardboard. Get creative! You have two weeks to finish it.'

'Bisi...' I stopped when I saw she was hurriedly packing her stuff. She shoved her things into her bag and walked away without a word.

I sighed and headed out of class towards the boarding grounds and dining hall. Students streamed eagerly past me, chatting and giggling. I never used to walk to lunch alone. The line at the dining hall wasn't long. I carried my tray of jollof rice and fried plantains to a far corner, avoiding our usual table. I didn't want to see who Bisi was having lunch with, didn't want to see Lanre. There was a free space at the last table in the hall where the junior students sat. They stared at me with big, worried eyes, so I tried to smile reassuringly. 'Is it okay if I sit here?'

Two girls nodded uncertainly. I had hardly seated myself when they were staring even more fearfully at someone behind me.

'Is it also okay if I join her?' It was Lanre's voice. My plantain fell off my fork and on to my plate. Was it normal for a single voice to melt all the joints that held a person's nerves together? 'I would love to keep her company, she looks so sad today.'

The girls giggled, one covering her mouth, her eyes wide and excited as she stared at Lanre. Still giggling and whispering, they shuffled together on the bench to make space opposite.

I glanced at him, immediately regretting it.

Hot waves shot through me. My face felt flushed and hot.

That smile.

Of course, the sides of my lips began twitching.

'The jollof rice is really good today,' he said.

I nodded, staring at my rice.

'Bisi not coming for lunch?' he asked.

I looked across to our usual table.

'She didn't come in today,' Lanre said.

'Oh,' I replied.

'Are you still not talking?'

I looked around the hall again. 'Well, she did say she wanted to talk, but I didn't react very nicely, I think, and then she ran off, so I … I thought she wanted to…'

'Run off for lunch without you?' He raised his eyebrows.

I felt foolish and mean.

'Seems like she isn't having any lunch at all today,' he said quietly.

I stared at my plate.

'Tara,' he said. I couldn't look up. 'Tara, we are here, you know. Your friends. Bisi has been missing you terribly. And I've been just as miserable.'

His voice was so gentle, he looked so earnest. My chest ached.

'I haven't been myself,' I murmured. 'I shouldn't... I can't... On Saturday I'm going to tell my parents that...' The words wouldn't come.

Lanre stretched out his hand and covered mine.

Giggling erupted beside us. The juniors were watching.

Lanre sighed and took his hand back.

'Let's talk later. Please.'

I nodded, my belly tight.

38

'Bisi, come back!'

The door of Mrs Abimbola's office burst open, slamming into the wall and Bisi stormed out.

I froze.

'You will not take matters into your own hands,' Mrs Abimbola called sharply. But Bisi didn't look like she was listening. Her face was contorted in anger as she dashed past, almost knocking me down. She stormed into Funmi 14 and I ran after her.

Two girls from Funmi 6 opposite followed us in.

There was scrambling and shouting as Bisi shoved Lola on to her bed, hitting her arm painfully on the ladder.

'You lying, wicked, devilish witch,' Bisi yelled.

Lola was up in an instant and tried to grab Bisi in a stranglehold. Bisi wriggled out of her grasp and they began pummelling each other on the floor.

Halima and Rosemary screamed from their bunks, but Chidinma jumped up and tried to separate them, retreating when she got a stray kick to her belly.

Lola grabbed Bisi from behind, jerking her head back with her plaits. Bisi cried out in pain and threw her weight into Lola, who toppled, crashing into a locker.

I had been standing in the doorway paralysed but I shook myself. 'Bisi! What are you doing?' I cried.

'She is a witch! A mean, dirty, lying witch.'

'What is your problem?' Lola screamed. 'Have you gone mad?'

'Where are your scissors?' Bisi yelled. She pinned Lola to the locker with her lower arm. 'Tell us where they are?'

Lola stared at her, eyebrows knitted to a frown. She was huffing and gasping for breath. A nasty-looking scratch on her forehead was turning purple.

'Why did you borrow Rosemary's scissors in art class today?'

'I misplaced mine,' Lola retorted. 'What's your business?'

'Leave her alone!' Mrs Abimbola's harsh voice cut through the room.

Bisi did not react.

'Bisi!' Mrs Abimbola said in a dangerously low voice. 'Don't make me repeat myself.'

I rushed forward and gripped Bisi's arm.

'Bisi, please,' I whispered. 'You are going to be in such serious trouble.'

Bisi let go and Lola slid dramatically to the ground, coughing and acting like she was dying.

'Now, get up, Lola, and stop all that show. Answer the question,' Mrs Abimbola said.

I stared at Mrs Abimbola along with everyone else. What had got into her and Bisi? What was so important about Lola having lost her scissors?

'I don't know. They went missing. I couldn't find them the other day.'

'Oh, just like that?' Bisi hissed. 'They disappeared by themselves?'

'Well, I don't know, probably someone snuck into my stuff and stole them,' Lola hissed back. 'What is your problem?'

'Bisi reported the missing scissors to me, when she saw Tara had her scissors in art class, but you didn't.'

I flinched at my name. What did I have to do with all this? I'd had enough attention these past few days. I did not need any more trouble.

Mrs Abimbola held up a nylon bag – long, fluffy clumps of hair could be seen through the plastic. A glint of metal caught my eye and my heart began to thud erratically.

'It was you! You're the one who cut off Salewa's hair!' Bisi yelled. 'We checked the scissors in the bag. They have your initials scratched into them!'

The room went silent as Mrs Abimbola pulled out the scissors and held them up. The doorway began filling with more girls.

Mrs Abimbola stared at Lola gravely. 'Have you got something to tell us?'

'Of course not, Ma! Why would I do such a thing?'

'Because you have been jealous of Tara since the first day she arrived. You have been after her every single day, teasing, making fun, just because you can't stand anyone being more popular than you.'

I could hardly breathe. Could this be true? Could...

'That's a lie,' Lola cried angrily. 'Chidinma also heard her shouting "cut off the hair" that night. Apart from that, we all know Tara likes to sleepwalk, doing who knows what kind of devilish things.'

'*That's* a lie,' Bisi yelled. 'She doesn't do any devilish things. That is your speciality!'

'Quiet!' Mrs Abimbola snapped. 'I repeat: Lola, why are your scissors in this bag?'

There was whispering at the door and Salewa walked in. She was wearing a dark blue durag to cover her bald head. To even out her hair, Mrs Abimbola had had to shave it completely. Against school rules, except if you were a Muslim, Mrs Abimbola had allowed her to cover her head.

'I don't know, Ma. Yes, I teased Tara a bit, but I think she wanted to get back at me, by framing me.

That's why she stole my scissors and left them there as proof.'

'What?' I cried, anger welling up inside. If it was true and Lola had really done this to Salewa and framed me, making me think I was going mad, then I was ready to slam her into the locker myself.

'If I had planned to frame you, why wouldn't I have called attention to the scissors?' I cried. 'Why would I have taken all that punishment and shame?'

'I know my rights,' Lola said, her face becoming cold. 'My dad is a lawyer. The scissors are no proof. Anyone could have taken them. What we do know for sure is that Tara was shouting about cutting off someone's hair all night and the bag was under *her* bed!'

She pointed at me and my heart sank.

'I can't believe you would frame me like this!' Lola's voice broke now and she began to sob.

'It's okay. No need for crying,' Mrs Abimbola said. She glanced at me with a frown, obviously unsure what to do. Salewa walked up to Lola and placed a hand on her heaving shoulder.

'I believe Lola,' Salewa said. 'Lola and I never had any issues, Mrs Abimbola. She wouldn't have had any reason to cut my beautiful hair.' Her lips wobbled as she touched the durag on her head. 'It was the longest hair in the entire school,' she sniffed.

Bisi hissed loudly. 'That sounds exactly like all the

motive Lola would need. Your hair was longer than hers. And, by the way, Tara also had no reason to cut your hair, Salewa. She hardly knew you.'

'Enough!' Mrs Abimbola said. 'I cannot blame Lola for having her scissors in a bag. If Tara says she cannot remember what happened...' Mrs Abimbola glanced at me and then at Bisi and shrugged. 'We will have to leave things as they are. Tara has already been punished, in any case.'

'No,' Bisi yelled. 'It is not fair! Tara would never do a thing like that! I know it was Lola!'

'Enough!'

Salewa was crying all over again.

I felt my body weaken and guilt come over me as everyone looked first at Salewa and then at me.

'Everyone back to their business,' Mrs Abimbola called and turned to leave.

'I know who did it!' a voice said quietly.

Rosemary was gripping the bed post, her face twisted in anger and fear. She was staring at Salewa crying into Lola's shoulder.

'I saw the person leave the room and come back to hide something under Tara's bed.'

Lola's face contorted with rage. 'Rosi! Don't you dare...'

'It was Lola,' Rosemary called loudly.

Salewa gasped and jumped back. 'I always knew you were jealous of me and my family because we have money. And because of my long hair.'

'Goodness, you are even sicker than I thought,' Lola hissed.

Mrs Abimbola walked up to Rosemary.

'Are you sure of what you are saying?' she asked grimly.

Rosemary glanced fearfully at Lola, but nodded. 'After Tara's screams, I couldn't sleep straight away. It had been really creepy. Lola waited till she thought everyone was asleep. Then she rummaged around in her things, I guess she must have been searching for her scissors, I couldn't see what it was. She was missing for about ten to fifteen minutes. I thought she'd gone to the toilet. When she came back, I heard a rustling sound as she kneeled in front of Tara's bed and slipped something underneath. Next morning, I had already forgotten about it. It was only when Lola said we should look for Salewa's hair that I realised what was going on.'

'So why did you not say anything, you stupid girl?' Mrs Abimbola asked, her eyebrows almost meeting in the middle of her forehead.

Rosemary moved away and glanced again at Lola.

In that moment Lola got up and flung herself at Rosemary. 'You snitch. After all I have done for you.'

Bisi and Chidinma grabbed Lola, pulling her off Rosemary who was trembling and pale.

'Lola! In my office right now!' Mrs Abimbola's voice was cold as ice. 'Rosemary! You too!'

The room was silent as they all marched out. No one spoke for at least a minute.

Bisi sank on to Lola's bed. She was watching me, her face intent, waiting for the truth to hit me.

Salewa came up and took my hand.

'I am so sorry,' she said. 'I can't believe what Lola did. Our families are actually meant to be friends.'

I nodded quickly, wishing everyone would leave. I needed a moment, needed to think.

But first I needed to…

I reached over to Bisi and pulled her into the tightest hug. She'd believed in me, even when I hadn't believed in myself.

39

'I am still a freak, though!'

Lanre cocked his head and looked at me closely through the fence. The light was fading and his eyes had a deep, warm glow.

'Only a freak would believe they could cut off someone's hair when they didn't.' I glanced back at Lola's silhouette in the almost dark field behind us. She had been given a patch of the larger field to cut since I had done the atrium. Lola's punishment was worse because the boys' dorm could catch glimpses of her through the fence. She had been cutting all afternoon, her pride and coolness disappearing with the sweat dripping down her face into her soaked PU.

'Who said I don't like freaks?' Lanre said. I could hear the grin in his voice.

'I can understand Yoruba. Just like that. Even though I never heard it before coming to Nigeria.'

'Oh, the genius kind of freaks, those are the best ones, you know.' His voice was slow and sexy and even though I wanted to keep him at a safe distance, I felt my resolve crumbling and my insides melting to hot jelly.

'I have nightmares where I sleepwalk, and sometimes I have no idea if I am dreaming or awake.'

'Have you ever kissed through a fence?' he asked. He had switched to Yoruba and I understood him perfectly. I shook my head, and found myself leaning in.

From far away, the dorm bell rang for dinner, but time didn't matter. Not when lips could be so soft and delicately entwined, causing the strangest of thrills.

'Hey,' he said tenderly. He pushed his hands through the gaps in the fence and took mine in his. 'I know it's tough, but don't allow what happens at night to take over your real life. The person in your dreams is not you. You are the person right here, right now. Here, you have control over yourself, and what you do.'

I looked into his eyes and wished I could believe him. The problem was, I felt my dreams were taking me somewhere and changing me along the way. And I had the feeling I could do nothing about it.

'All right?' he asked.

I nodded.

'As for Lola, just ignore her. She is...' He paused. 'Complicated.'

'You seem to know her well?'

'Not really. Wale, my friend, the one who let you use his phone to call the commission?'

I nodded.

'He's good friends with her cousin, Theo.'

That wasn't much of an explanation. Lanre seemed vague all of a sudden, as if he was keeping something from me. I remembered him smiling at Lola and giving her the Coke he'd got for me. My belly tightened and I realised I was jealous.

What did he know and why wasn't he telling?

40

'**M**ama, why do they want to build up the city wall so quickly?' Ofeefee asked. She dropped the oil lantern, wiping sweat off her face with the back of her hand. Muddy fingers left a brown streak on her pale forehead.

'Yes, why the hurry?' Dudu heaved the large wooden tray with the dried mud brick off her head with a groan. She stretched her back and neck. 'See how people are hurrying around like hens in a panic. As if the Egun themselves have left their spirit realm and are planning a visit.' Her green eyes gleamed wickedly in the limpid greyness of the fading night.

Ofeefee giggled. 'Not that these old city walls would keep anybody out. Definitely not spirits. The walls are brittle and ruined and even if we repair these at Aro, what about the walls on the northern side?'

'Be quiet, both of you!' their mother warned, glancing around nervously. Dark shadows hurried past, bearing bowls of mud, ropes, vines and branches. 'We do not want any trouble,' she continued. 'We will do our share here and then we will be gone. I do not want you drawing attention to us. Have you understood me?'

'Yes, Mama,' they replied together, lowering their eyes.

Their mother sighed and came closer. She held one twin in each arm and whispered, 'My daughters, I heard there is to be an attack. A spy sent a message to Abeokuta saying King Gezo of a place called Dahomey has sent his warriors. They were sighted at Ishaga and they are coming to fight the Egba people. The Alake himself ordered the repair of the walls. If they break in, if they win, you know what will happen.'

'They will steal us to sell as slaves to the white men waiting on the large waters,' Ofeefee replied, her voice a whisper.

Dudu pulled herself out of her mother's grasp, eyes glowing with anger. 'Why should we help them?' she hissed. 'When it is festival time or storytelling or sharing of yam, they ignore us like we are beasts. But now, when they are afraid and need help for their useless wall, they call us to join in and work with them.'

'Shh!' her mother warned. 'Bind your anger, my child, and be careful what you say. We are different and they do not know how to behave towards us, that is all.'

'They treat us like dirt,' Dudu spat. 'They say we are witches that walk in the night doing evil things!'

'And remember what they nearly did to us?' Ofeefee said, her eyes fearful.

The mother caressed her daughter's short hair, sighing. The memory of the attempted sacrifice at the rock was still fresh in their minds.

'I know. It is just for now, until...' She stopped, and the twins glanced at each other uneasily.

The mother was looking towards the rock in the distance. Its foothills were still veiled in the greyness of dawn, casting a shadow over the hundreds of houses at its base. But the top of the rock glowed orange and majestic under the first touch of sun. 'As long as we are close to the rock, we will be safe,' she said. 'The power of the rock will protect us.'

There were shouts from beyond the wall and a young man ran in.

'Egba warriors,' he called. 'Egba warriors, get up and fight. They have arrived! They have reached the river!'

Two women swinging empty water pots and gasping for breath followed, screaming, 'They are coming, oh! We saw the warriors near Ogun River!'

The men setting the bricks into the wall climbed up frantically to see. 'Beat the drums! Beat the drums of warning,' they yelled.

'Mama!' the girls called as she darted away. 'What are you doing?' Their mother was running towards the wall, and as she ran, her head tie loosened and fell to the ground. Ofeefee snatched it up. Dudu grabbed her hand and they hurried after their mother.

A young man jumped off the wall and ran past them, back towards the huts. He was mumbling the strange language of the white man from the mission. 'Oh Lord, have mercy on us, protect us. Oh Lord, have mercy on us, protect us.'

'I must see,' their mother gasped, as she climbed up the bamboo ladder. She moved carefully along the wall towards the hole that had still not been fixed.

The twins followed, squeezing past men who stood rigidly, as if their feet were stuck to the floor with rubber-tree sap.

The snaking shape of the Ogun River could be seen clearly now. The sun had almost fully risen, spreading soft morning light from Olumo's foothills, over the cluster of houses and all the way across the plains up to the river. At first it resembled a thin trail of brown honey dotted with hundreds of ants. Only the river was not honey and the dots were not ants. They were hundreds of warriors crossing the river in swarms. And behind them, a wall of hundreds more waited their turn.

It was dry season and the river was parched and low. They waded through easily, arms raised to keep safe their shiny machetes, guns and bows and arrows.

'Will it hold?' the twins asked, as they stretched their necks and toes to see, gripping the folds of their mother's wrapper with trembling hands. 'Will the wall hold?'

But the mother did not reply. Her eyes were distant and she was shaking her head and mumbling incantations. The warriors who had crossed the river charged forward, chanting war cries in high-pitched, aggressive voices. Their faces, painted red and black, looked distorted, giving them a monstrous appearance.

Closer and closer they came, with long, angry strides.

41

'Seems like I am not the only one breaking rules in Funmi 14,' a low voice said.

My heart jumped in fright, and I bumped my head against the bar of lovers' window.

Lola was sitting on the dirt ground outside. Hidden in the shadows, she'd watched me huff and squeeze my bum out all this while without saying a word.

She was holding a cigarette, puffing creamy smoke into the night air.

I peered out into the darkness. My limbs were bristling with the familiar urge. Leafy silhouettes danced in front of me and I grabbed the window ledge, dizzy with the energy sizzling in my veins. I couldn't see the rock from here, but I could sense its presence through the night, beckoning me.

Lola was watching. Waiting.

What the hell was I supposed to say?

'I thought it was a perfect night to see the stars.'

She raised an eyebrow, the disbelief in her face briefly lit by the orange glow of her cigarette.

'It's the Harmattan season, girl. You ain't gonna see no stars up there,' she drawled.

I glanced up and saw she was right. The sky was overcast with a fog-like veil.

There was a moment of silence – only the sound of crickets and the chill wind echoed through the treetops.

'It's like tearing off a straitjacket … that's what an open sky does. Especially in this place,' she said.

I glanced at her, unsure if she was making fun of me. But she was deadly serious. Her face didn't have its usual hard, cynical look. She seemed lost in thought.

Another cold gust swept viciously round us and the way it swirled, almost angrily, its currents electrifying and sweeping through my thin nightwear, was like hissing spirits.

I rubbed my arms. Why hadn't I put on a sweater? It was more biting than I thought possible in Nigeria. Since the Harmattan winds had come, the air felt different – dry, brittle and strangely alive.

'Talking about straitjackets, some good advice for Harmattan season: never go outside at night without a jacket.' The sarcasm was definitely back.

'Yeah,' I mumbled. I peered wistfully through the bushes, but it didn't seem like I was going anywhere tonight. What had come over me anyway? My determination had fizzed out and I felt tired beyond words.

I sighed and leaned into the wall. I might as well admire the night sky, even if it was starless.

Lola took a pull on her cigarette. 'So, what brought you out here? Bad dreams?'

I shuddered at the memory of the approaching warriors chanting their war song, eyes and veins bulging, fuming with a fanatic mission. I had woken and heaved up my dinner in the bathroom. Had Lola heard?

With shaky hands, I had studied the drawings in Omi's sketchbook by the light of my torch. Tracing the faces of Ofeefee and Dudu and the fine slashes of pencil that Omi had drawn around their mother's neck. The chain with its intricate symbols and the leopard staring out of them.

It just didn't make sense.

The wind outside had grown stronger and the distant moaning had crept into the room. I'd dropped the sketchbook and from one moment to the next, found myself slipping through lovers' window.

'Or was it our howling spirit yonder that called you?' Lola continued. 'I was just thinking I should save my wretched niash and go back in when you rushed out to meet it.'

Did Lola guess how true her words were?

'Why are *you* out here?' I asked, more aggressively than I'd intended.

'Tomorrow is parents' visiting day.'

I knew what that meant. Mrs Abimbola was going to have a long talk with Lola's parents. She'd yelled it loud enough for all the dorms to hear.

I didn't envy her but she wouldn't get my sympathy. What she had done was really wicked.

I snatched a glance at her. Maybe I could get her to talk about Omi…

She held out her cigarette.

'No, thanks,' I said but slid down beside her.

'Tss…' She let out a half-laugh. 'Of course Miss Perfect London doesn't smoke.' The sneer was back and I immediately regretted sitting down with her.

I didn't reply.

'Salewa deserved what she got, you know.'

'Is that what you think?'

'She is a rich snob of a brat and she was one of those who treated Omi like shit and spread rumours about her. She had it coming.'

I held my breath. This was going better than expected.

'What rumours?'

Lola puffed out circles of smoke without replying.

'Was Omi a friend of yours?'

Lola didn't answer and I sighed in frustration.

'What about me?' I asked, changing tack. 'Why did I deserve punishment for a crime you committed? Why have you been on my case since I arrived?'

She shrugged. 'You are also one of those privileged brats who doesn't even know it. Do you realise how much the school fees we pay here are? Have you ever looked two metres outside at the hawking kids selling kola nuts at the gate?'

Her eyes pierced mine and she went on.

'Did you stop to think why a ten-year-old kid is selling kola nuts and not in school?'

I swallowed. Of course I'd noticed, but I'd kind of accepted it as normal in Nigeria.

'I'm fully aware life does not share its giveaways equally,' she continued. 'But can those who get the big fat prizes at least appreciate their position and remember the ones who drew the blanks?'

'So what, you are the holy Lola, living the meek life and oozing sympathy for those less fortunate? Come on, you are just as privileged if you are at this school,' I lashed back.

She looked at me, her eyes on fire. 'That's not the point. You stroll around, living the life, spreading your London vibes and all, not caring about anything around you. And that sucks!'

'This sounds like you are blaming me for being myself? Sorry I'm from England. Sorry that bothers you. I can't change it!'

'You don't even get it. At least you have the privilege of just being yourself! That's more than some people have!'

She spat the words out so bitterly I turned to face her. 'Sorry, but I don't buy this. You are not making any sense. If anyone here is doing exactly what they feel like without caring about consequences, it's you.'

'I can do everything I want, except the one thing...'

She stopped talking and drew a long, ragged breath. 'I can't wait to be out of here. Out of this ... this temple of fakeness. Out of this damn fake country! I can't believe people like you actually want to come here.' She spoke through gritted teeth.

Lola took one last pull on her cigarette, then pressed the stump into the ground with enough force to bury it.

I wanted to ask what she meant, what had made her so spiteful, but she got up abruptly.

'If I were you, I wouldn't stay out here alone.'

I threw one last wistful glance into the backyard, but the moment was gone and I was chilled to the bone. The trees seemed menacing, the bushes wild.

'Things have been known to happen in this school. Evil things.'

She moved aside, making space for me to go first.

I waited for her to say more, but it was as if those words had sealed her lips.

42

'What the... Tara, look straight ahead at the serving ladies,' Bisi hissed as we queued for breakfast. 'Second from left!'

My eyes widened as I took in Lola wearing a hair net and serving food. She looked like she was trying to slap students with the slice of bread she was flinging on to their plates. Chunks of fried egg were scattered around her.

'Okay, I think this is the worst punishment I have seen so far,' Bisi whispered. 'Cutting grass in front of your dorm is bad enough but this ... face to face with the entire school, including the boys. And wearing that hair net!'

'Yeah, the hair net's the worst,' I agreed.

'Not that she doesn't deserve it!' Bisi said grimly.

We had hardly been seated and said prayers when Mrs Abimbola walked into the dining hall, wearing a grey suit and white blouse.

'Quiet, everyone, please!' she called. 'I have a brief announcement to make.'

'It's Saturday! Why is she dressed like that?' I whispered.

'You mean, so officially?' Bisi asked.

'Because it's parents' visiting day,' Lanre said, not looking up from his toast he was loading with scrambled eggs.

'Oh,' I said, with a sigh of relief when I remembered that didn't apply to me.

'She is going to act like the most amazing and compassionate dorm mistress that ever walked the boarding school grounds of this earth,' Bisi added.

Mrs Abimbola looked in our direction with lips pressed tightly together. We went quiet.

'I have an announcement to make concerning the night noises that some students have been complaining about.'

The toast slipped out of my hands on to my plate.

'Security guards searched the entire premises for hours last night…'

I gulped. If Lola hadn't been out there, the security guards would have caught me. What punishment would I have received? My hands had only just stopped hurting from the first time.

'I can assure everyone they did not find any bush babies, ghosts, witches or other night creatures,' Mrs Abimbola continued with a raised eyebrow.

There was snickering around the hall.

'So those of you who suffer from a hyper-imagination can begin the process of calming down.' Mrs Abimbola placed her hands on her hips and looked around sternly. 'Like I have told those girls who came to me crying and panicking: there is no Haven ghost – as some of you have named it – haunting us here. We do not have spirits in our school.'

She hadn't said spirits did not exist, only that we didn't have one. We knew she believed in them and had often prayed for our protection against dark forces.

'The security guards found out where the night noises have been coming from.' The hall was dead quiet. Even the boys who didn't hear anything on their side cocked their heads in anticipation. 'They found a cave underneath a rock on the edge of the premises.'

Beside me, Bisi breathed in sharply. 'Our secret spot,' she whispered. But I was too astonished to speak. That was exactly where I had wanted to go last night. I had felt it in my bones, that painful throb urging me out of the window.

'The mouth of this cave faces the river, and the wind blowing across the river and into the cave causes some kind of friction. This is what makes the strange sounds.'

Students began discussing in hushed tones.

A girl raised her hand.

'Yes, Caroline?' Mrs Abimbola asked.

'Why did the wailing stop these past months? Why did it start again now?'

'Very good question. We think this is connected to the season change. Bushes might have grown to cover the mouth of the cave and the heavy rains may have swelled the river and ripped away those bushes blocking the cave. Another idea is that the Harmattan season has brought stronger winds.'

A lot of murmuring followed.

Mrs Abimbola glanced towards the door and nodded.

Three men approached. Two were wearing a black-and-grey security uniform. I recognised one as the guard at the gate who had allowed me to buy the kola nuts.

They were tall and bulky, as you would expect, and swaggered in boldly. The third looked more scraggly and out of place beside them. He wore a faded white kaftan and a little white cap on his head which he kept rearranging and patting down. He didn't look like he was feeling this moment of standing in front of a mass of students. 'These young men here were so kind as to search the premises,' Mrs Abimbola said. 'Please tell the students, did you see any spirits out there?'

The security guards both grinned and shook their heads.

The hunched man pulled off his cap, and was looking at his feet. He was wearing flip-flops and his long, scrawny toes bulged over the sides.

'Who is the third guy they forced to come along?' I whispered.

'That's the gardener. He hardly speaks English. Probably doesn't even know what's going on,' Bisi replied.

I thought of the well-kept garden hidden behind the school that was out of bounds for everyone, with the strange shadows flitting through it.

He hadn't nodded his head like the other two men.

'In any case, you have your explanation,' Mrs Abimbola was saying. 'I do not want to hear any more nonsense about this issue. It is forbidden for anybody to come knocking on my door in the middle of the night to tell me about crying witches or wailing monsters. Everybody will calm down and stop the scary talk. Cross the Haven ghost out of your minds. Have I made myself clear?'

'Yes, Ma!' the hall rumbled in response.

'Perfect timing,' Lanre said. 'Let's sort out the ghost before parents arrive.'

'We don't want students howling or begging to be taken home like last time,' Wale cut in.

'Your mum coming?' Lanre asked Bisi gently.

Bisi nodded, her mouth full of toast.

'I'm glad she'll make it,' Lanre said.

'Well, it's a big sacrifice, but, yes, last minute, she said she would "pop by" briefly.'

'Next important point,' Mrs Abimbola continued. 'I want the dorms to be in top form today. Every single girl will look shiny and bright, every uniform flawlessly ironed and every bed perfectly made. Not a single piece of paper anywhere. I am sure you all want to show yourselves at your best!'

Mrs Abimbola gave the men a nod and they retreated.

'Now go on, eat up! In just a few hours you will be seeing your families.'

'Yayy!' Cries went through the dining hall and everyone began talking in feverish voices.

But I couldn't share the excitement. I didn't believe Mrs Abimbola. I had felt the call of the rock in my very bones.

I watched the gardener through the window. He was hurrying towards the little locked gate, shoulders hunched, and his cap clutched tight in his hand.

He knew it. I was sure of it. He knew the cry was not the wind.

43

The dorm was as quiet as a graveyard. Since coming to Olumo Haven I had not had a single moment of quiet like this. The girls had run off to the reception area to wait for their parents and those whose parents lived too far away from Abeokuta for a mid-term visit were in the phone-call room. I flung my mobile on my bunk and tried to ignore it. Mrs Abimbola had given me a sympathetic smile.

'You can talk for as long as you like during visiting hours, dear,' she'd said. Since Lola had been exposed, she had been especially nice to me. 'Make a video call, okay?' she'd added with an awkward wink that definitely didn't suit her, followed by a clumsy pat on my shoulder.

'Thank goodness I didn't get around to informing your parents about the unfortunate hair incident,' she'd said. 'No reason getting them worked up about it now, is there?' She'd stood waiting for an answer and

I'd nodded quickly, feeling disgusted. Not that I'd have wanted to discuss that with Mum and Dad. They were worried enough as it is.

I stared at the phone in my hand, my fingers not moving to make the call.

Instead I grabbed one of the novels I'd found in the common room and tried to read. The cover said *Treasure Island* by Robert Louis Stevenson, but the story had nothing to do with treasure, ships or maps. It was about Lady Waverley, her castle and a tall, handsome visitor.

But my mind kept straying to my dream the night before. The warriors, the vicious faces, the chanting. The mother and her twins, watching in horror.

I jerked upright in my bunk, Lady Waverley and *Treasure Island* crashing to the floor, and I was breathing hard. I had a name. A name from my dream. A king, whose warriors had come to attack the Egba people. The mother had told the twins that King Gezo had sent them. What if … if that name really existed? It might connect my dreams to real life!

I jumped out of bed, but fell back with a sigh.

Argh! The library was closed because everyone was going berserk about their parents visiting.

I groaned in frustration.

Had the guide at Olumo Rock mentioned King Gezo when she talked about the Egba wars? I couldn't remember anything. If he had really existed, I could connect my dreams to a specific date in the past. It would be the proof I needed that it was not all in my imagination. That I wasn't going mad!

I bent over to pick up Lady Waverley and saw that my phone had fallen down with it. I pressed the *On* button and sighed in relief when the screen lit up.

The bright round search engine caught my eye. I squealed.

Stupid me! I had free internet access all afternoon and hadn't even realised it.

The answers came up immediately, wiping away each and every doubt.

I read fast, gulping down all the information I could find:

Gezo was the King of Dahomey, now known as the republic of Benin, from 1818 to 1858. His forty-year reign was notorious for its cruelty. He instilled terror in neighbouring regions which he ravaged to reclaim territories and capture slaves for sale to European merchants. He was highly involved in the slave trade, even though this inhuman business had been recently abolished. His rule was defined by several important military victories, many of which were executed in the Yorubaland of current day Nigeria. Abeokuta, which had been founded as a safe haven for people

during wars and against slave raiding in an easily
defended location at the foot of Olumo Rock, became
one of King Gezo's targets. He attacked Abeokuta in
1851 and 1864.

My heart pounded so loudly and my hands shook so
badly I had to draw several long breaths to calm myself.
This was it! My dreams were visions from the mid-
nineteenth century! How mind-blowing was that? I
continued reading.

Gezo was credited with the formation of a brutal and
fierce female military regiment, the Mino, popularly
called 'the Amazons' by Europeans. Although female
bodyguards had existed for many kings before him,
it was Gezo who transformed them into a force for
battle; the most ferocious female warriors ever seen
on the continent. They took delight in the collection
of skulls of their enemies.

My mind was a mess. Ruth had drawn bloody,
dismembered heads and skulls in her diary. Omi had also
drawn a bloodcurdling portrait of one of the warriors.

Ofeefee, Dudu and their mother had watched the
warriors cross the Ogun River. That had truly happened.
I had seen it.

Had they survived the attack?

My belly twisted in fear for them.

And for myself.

This was more proof. I dreamed of real events that had taken place in the past. Now remained one important question:

Why?

44

I fetched Ruth's little blue diary and Omotara's sketchbook which I had hidden behind some clothes in my locker. I had to find out what the connection was. Between Omotara and me, the chain, the visions and Ruth, there had to be something I had overlooked until now. I turned the pages of Ruth's diary, the incoherent sentences, as usual, making me turn the pages quicker. I tried my best to ignore the pain radiating from her confused words, the terror transmitted by her jagged, unfinished sketches.

King's women bring death.

Yes, that had to be King Gezo of Dahomey!

A demon without colour, was scrawled next. What did that mean?

As I turned the pages, some of the words jumped out, and now seemed to make sense.

Broken walls ... build up the city walls...

Death waded through the river...

There were skulls everywhere, littered across pages.

We had shared the same visions. They had haunted her, like they haunted me.

The memory of my grandfather's words sent a chill down my spine: *For over one hundred and fifty years, every female Bensworth has lived a cursed life. Each one died at their own hand.*

I picked up Omi's sketchbook and began flicking through. When I reached her last drawing, I continued turning the empty pages in frustration. To my surprise, I found one final drawing at the end.

It was Lola's face.

She had captured her in a dreamy moment. There was no sign of the usual hardness. She was beautiful.

I stared at the sketch, absolutely confused. What was Lola's role in all this? What did she know? She had acted so strangely about the chain and had been so unwilling to speak about Omi.

I sighed. I would have to try again. Maybe Lola was the missing puzzle piece in all this.

I hid the books under my pillow and walked out of the dorm. I was tired of sitting around and pondering. I needed to *do* something. Apart from Lola, who was probably with her parents now, my only other lead was the secret cave with its eerie moans. Those weren't some Harmattan winds causing air friction in a cave. Maybe I would finally get an answer.

I hurried out of the dorm. The bustling, joyful scene in our field was annoying. Chattering girls strolled with their parents and visiting siblings, full of excited talk, takeaway bags of fast food, cakes and other treats.

I waited for a good moment to slip around our building, when Mrs Abimbola appeared. She walked past me with a grave expression, not looking in my direction. She was talking to a smart, older couple. It was only then I noticed Lola walking behind with a stony face.

'We can go into my office and discuss the further disciplinary measures we feel would be necessary to ensure she is back on the right track,' Mrs Abimbola was saying. 'My students are close to my heart. Especially students like Lola, whom I try to guide with special attention.' She sounded quite caring – maybe she was nicer than we thought? If only she didn't have such outdated principles...

'She has always been a rather difficult child. That is why we sent her to boarding school,' her father said.

Lola caught sight of me and glared me into the ground before going in after them.

I wondered how I was ever going to have a decent conversation with her.

One last glance, then I slipped through the bushes beside the dorm and out of sight.

By the time I reached the rock, I was out of breath.

I heaved myself up with the help of the fence, then lay flat on top of the rock, gasping for air. When I had calmed, I crawled forward till I was at the very edge, overlooking the river.

The entrance to the cave was dark and covered with shrubs, with the fast swirling river running in front of it. The current was strong and chances of falling in and being swept away were high.

It wasn't going to be easy.

I felt foolish. What was I doing here? Right now, I didn't feel any connection to this place. A flash of silver-grey swam past and I followed the slalom trail of the fish until they were gone. The river was dull, reflecting the faded sky. The clouds seemed heavy with red dust, blocking any view of the sun. Since the Harmattan winds had come, the dust had taken over everything, giving the air a constant hazy, almost foggy feel. A thin film of red covered every surface. Even the rock I was lying on was coated in it.

I wiped my hands, resting my chin on them and watched the water rush past. The river stretched ahead, then curved out of sight. I could feel Olumo's eyes on me and on the river, watching it make its swift journey around the city. I remembered the terrifying warriors holding their glistening weapons above their heads as they splashed through the water. Where had they crossed? It could have been in this very spot. I felt overwhelmed, scared even. The gulping sounds of the river seemed to be getting louder.

I scrambled back, feeling a chill move up my arms. A malicious wind licked my skin with its cold, dry tongue. It gathered in strength and the river swirled wildly. Whispers began to creep from below, gathering in intensity, until they reached a terrible pitch that ripped out from the cave. It was heartrending and pulsated through the rock beneath me and into my bones.

'Hey! You there! Commot for there!'

A thin man with a cutlass and a rake was standing between some trees close to the staff quarters. The gardener! He was waving me down.

I slid from the rock, feeling dazed and wobbly on my feet. Stumbling away, I ran through the fruit orchard with the orange trees, through the bushes and the maize farm towards the back of the dorm.

'Hey! Come back hia! Nonsense pickin!' he called.

But I had no intention of getting caught.

45

I was speeding around the dorm, giddy with relief at having escaped the gardener, when I almost ran into a grim-looking Mrs Abimbola in the doorway.

'Where were you?'

'Ehm… I went for a short walk … to the dining hall and back,' I lied.

'I can't believe this.' Mrs Abimbola placed her hands on her hips. 'I was in the middle of a meeting when I was informed your parents were waiting for your call, worried something had happened. And you were strolling around? I even said you could keep the phone all afternoon! I don't understand.'

'Well … I did try calling, but they didn't pick up.' I was surprised by how easily the lies came.

'You couldn't try again a few minutes later?' Mrs Abimbola shook her head.

I tried to look remorseful, hoping to escape any more preaching.

'Well, hurry up and call them now.' She waved me away. 'I need to get back to my meeting. And bring me the phone when you have finished.'

She shook her head, again, mumbling. 'These children of nowadays. In my time, we had respect. Respect for our parents. Respect for our elders.'

I hurried to my dorm wondering what excuse I could give them for not calling, and how quickly I could get away.

—

'Lola! Can we talk?'

I stepped out from behind the pillars at the dining hall entrance. I had been hiding in wait for almost half an hour.

She looked tired after her evening shift serving dinner and washing plates and her face turned mad at the sight of me.

'I know I am the last person you want to see at the moment, but I really need to speak with you.'

'You are right. You are the last person I want to see!' She left me standing there and walked on.

'Lola, please!' I cried, running after her. 'It's about Omi!'

She flinched at the name, but continued walking.

'I know her name is Omotara,' I said hurriedly.

'Which is a strange coincidence, don't you think, considering I have her bunk?'

Lola glanced at me, but didn't stop. She was walking faster now and looked around at the shadows gathering in the corners of the field. She seemed worried. Scared, even.

'I know this might sound weird, but I think there is some connection between me and Omotara. I don't know what it is, but you see, I'm trying to find out things about my past. That's the reason I came to Nigeria. My search brought me here. To this school, to the same bunk in which a girl with a similar name slept and had the same dreams that I did.'

Lola stopped and whirled around. 'How do you know that?' Her eyes were large. She was afraid of me, I realised.

'I ... ehm ... I found her sketchbook. She drew people I have seen in my nightmares.'

Lola frowned.

'She also had nightmares, right?'

Lola nodded.

'You seem to know her quite well?'

Lola was wary again. She shrugged.

We had reached the entrance to the dorm. I pulled the drawing from Omi's sketchbook out of my rucksack. 'I found this picture of you.'

Lola stared at it. At first her face was blank, totally void of emotion. Then it convulsed into a painful twist and a tear rolled down her cheek. She began to gasp for breath and I became worried someone would hear.

'Let's go to the bench under those trees,' I whispered.

She followed me with hunched, heaving shoulders. I hoped nobody was at the wall tonight, so we would have some privacy to talk.

We sat down and I allowed her some minutes to calm herself. She kept looking at the sheet of paper in the dim light of the street lamp.

I caught sight of Lola's profile, the softness of her eyes in the drawing and suddenly, I understood the truth.

'You and Omi were more than just friends, weren't you?' I asked gently.

At first she didn't reply. But after some seconds she nodded.

'Nobody cared about her, you know. She was one of those people who was always completely ignored. People forgot she was in the room because she was quiet and reserved. But ... not me. She was clever, had a big heart and she was beautiful.'

She glanced at me uneasily. 'Seeing you walk in on your first day with all your shine-shine, brand new luggage and your British accent made me angry. You even look a bit like her. When you said your name, something in me cracked. It was as if you felt you had every right to take her place. You have everything she didn't. She was so poor and alone in this world!' She glared at me. 'I couldn't stand it.'

'I'm sorry,' I said.

'It's not your fault,' she said with a sour laugh. 'I'm the one who should be apologising. I have been quite a beast, haven't I?'

There was an awkward silence.

'Why did she leave?'

Lola snorted.

'Mrs Abimbola caught us.' She stared at her fingers, which she was kneading nervously. 'We were … ehm … entangled … and kissing in the bathroom. It was dead of night, of course, everyone was asleep. Or so we thought.'

She curled her fingers into a fist. 'It's so unfair! Having to hide from others. From yourself. Having to be … ashamed.' She spat the words as if she were disgusted, even with herself.

Suddenly the things she had said that night outside made sense. Her bitterness, her talk of the privilege of being oneself.

'If you knew how *much* I hate this stupid fence!' She waved her hand at it.

I looked at the wall, not understanding.

'Everybody is so excited to come here, to gawk at the boys on the other side, talk to them giggling, kiss them.'

She swallowed angrily.

'I … I can't ever like anybody on that side of the fence. They would be on *this* side and that is absolutely unimaginable.'

To think she had to listen to Mrs Abimbola's horrible prayer every morning. For Mrs Abimbola, a girl in Olumo Haven having a boyfriend was almost the highest crime. I heard a girl and a boy had been condemned to cut grass for a week for being caught kissing after class and then were suspended for two weeks. Two girls would be a catastrophe! I didn't even want to imagine what Mrs Abimbola's reaction had been when she caught Lola and Omi.

'I am in a prison here, on my side of the fence. Can you understand?' She glanced at me and Lola, who was always so tough, so self-confident, now looked like a lost little girl.

I nodded.

'I feel like a wolf in sheep's clothing, invading everyone's privacy, just by being who I am.' She paused. 'I never allowed myself to like anyone, you know. Until Omi...' Her voice broke. She drew a long breath and began to speak, very matter of fact. 'Mrs Abimbola immediately expelled Omi.'

'Only Omi?' I asked, confused.

Lola laughed bitterly and nodded. 'My parents are rich and important sponsors, etcetera, etcetera. Omi was a nobody. She was here on a scholarship. I only got some punishments. Not even too terrible because Mrs Abimbola was afraid the reason would come out if it was severe. And that would have been bad for her reputation, I guess, and the end of mine. So, she twisted the story, saying that Omi forced me.'

I stared at Lola in horror.

She sighed. 'Welcome to Olumo Haven. I can hardly wait to leave this place. Like I told you, I hate all these rich kids and their privileges. Most of them are disgusting. We once had an outing where everyone was allowed to wear mufti and Salewa and her friends spent the whole trip making comments about people's clothes. As if owning Louis Vuitton or Dsquared or whatever should be the primary goal of human life. They made fun of Omi, yelling across the entire bus to ask what brand her shoes were. When she ignored them, they said her shoes were Abeokuta local brand. Everyone on the bus found it so funny. Just not Omi. And not me.' She folded her arms across her chest and hissed.

'And I could never openly protect her. She wouldn't allow it because she was worried about the consequences for me. She never cared about anything happening to her. *I don't have a family who cares but you do*, she would say. So we even kept our friendship a secret, meeting only at night to whisper for hours in the bathroom.' Lola's voice broke and I gave her a moment.

'Did Omi ever tell you about her dreams?'

Lola shook her head. 'She was too terrified to talk about them. She had nightmares, but she didn't wake up screaming all over people's ears like you do.'

Lola raised an eyebrow at me. I squirmed and smiled ruefully.

'She used to wake up quietly and walk the corridors because she was afraid of sleeping. That's how we became friends. One night I went to the bathroom and found her pacing in tears.'

I felt sorry for Omi and could well understand her terror.

'She worried she was possessed, that there was some sort of magic involved.' Lola paused and looked at me. 'When I hear you at night, it sounds like the exact same thing is happening. You should be careful. The whole thing was getting to Omi. It consumed her. By the time Mrs Abimbola caught us, she was hardly herself any more.'

A cold wind blew around us and I rubbed my arms.

'Did she ever tell you why she thought she had the dreams? What they meant?'

Lola shook her head. 'When you came and also started having nightmares, I wondered if it was your bunk bed. Like, is it haunted or something?'

'No, I had the nightmares before I arrived at Olumo Haven. They brought me here.'

My heart sank down to my belly. Lola didn't know more.

'Where is Omi now? I would like to contact her.'

Lola began to shake her head frantically. She hid her face in her hands.

A terrible feeling came over me. 'What is it?'

'Omi is dead,' she whispered. 'She was found, drowned at the river behind the dorm, beside that rock that sits over the cave. Where the wailing noises come from at night.'

My mouth fell open.

'I was…' Lola almost chocked. 'I was the one who found her. It was the night before she was meant to leave. She had already packed, but wanted to go to her secret spot one last time. She'd been gone for hours and I slipped through lovers' window to look for her.'

I covered my mouth and felt tears rolling down my face. My fingers slid down over the chain and to my chest. A terrible pain burned inside me.

That was the spot I had found the broken pendant! My mind was racing. Poor Omi. Had she lost the pendant the night she died?

'How did it happen?' I managed finally.

'I don't know. Her foot was caught in some reeds, but her body was in the river. The water can be quite strong, especially in rainy season. She couldn't pull herself out, not against the current. It was probably an accident.'

'That's horrible,' I said.

'But that is not all,' Lola spat through tightly clenched teeth. Her eyes were so full of hate and pain it was difficult to look into them.

'Omi had no family, just a distant relative in a

faraway village who could not read or write and hardly knew her. Her dad abandoned them when she was little and her mum had killed herself. She had grown up in an orphanage.'

I gasped at this new parallel between Omi's life and my own, but Lola pushed on.

'Mrs Abimbola covered up the whole thing! She announced to everyone that Omi had left at dawn.'

'What?'

'She got rid of Omi's body with the help of a security guard, I think. They just threw her into the river like she was nothing!'

'Oh my god.'

'Next day they put up the gate leading to the orchard and said no one was allowed there any more.'

Lola let out a forced laugh. 'Then Mrs Abimbola made me swear never to mention Omi's name again or I would be publicly exposed and disgraced for homosexuality.'

'But why?' I cried, horrified. 'It's so outrageous! Why would she do such a thing?'

'Because on her watch nobody is allowed to be gay and on her watch nobody is allowed to die!'

46

Ofeefee closed her ears to the noise. The screams of children, the prayers and chants of the women, the terrible din of gunshots. They cracked through the air again and again and again, leaving grey smoke above and red death on the ground. Destruction was everywhere as the sun beat down mercilessly.

Dudu clutched her sister's hand tightly in hers. They huddled, crouched behind a hut, far from the southern city wall where King Gezo's warriors attacked.

'Stay here,' their mother said. 'I have to join the women carrying water and gunpowder to the men at the front.'

'No, Mama, I am scared,' Ofeefee said. 'Please stay!'

'I have to,' their mother said.

'You do not owe them anything. Why will you not see that?' Dudu cried in frustration.

'I am not doing it because I owe them anything. I am

doing it because I want a future here for both of you. I want them to accept you as one of them. If I do not help, someone will notice and later, who knows...'

'They will never accept us, Mother,' Dudu hissed. 'We are outcasts, monstrosities of nature. We have eyes the colour of a leopard. Ofeefee and I are like day and night although we are ibeji.'

'Stop it, Dudu,' Ofeefee cried.

Their mother tightened her wrapper around her waist and turned to leave.

'Tell us, Mother! Do we even have a human father? Or are we the result of one of your juju incantations like people say?'

Ofeefee gasped and shot a hand to cover Dudu's mouth.

Their mother stopped in her stride.

'Tell us, Mother! Are we an abomination – the children of a spirit leopard with green eyes? Ofeefee the yellow of his fur and I the colour of his spots?'

Their mother's face hardened, but as always, she did not reply to questions about their father. She hurried off to the women and children jostling and yelling around the hut that stored the gunpowder.

The twins watched her disappear into the din and smoke.

There were cries at the wall. 'They are climbing through! They are breaking through! Help us!'

Heavily muscled figures wielding machetes jumped nimbly over the wall. The warriors were painted all over in red and black, baring their teeth and scowling, as they swung their weapons. Their war cries were high-pitched and ear-splitting. Round-looking gourds hanging at their waists clacked noisily against each other.

'Those are not gourds!' Dudu cried. 'They have skulls tied to their belts!'

The Egba men fought furiously, but it was difficult to see who was winning through the rush of bodies.

Arrows soared over the wall and several people fell.

'God of Olumo Rock, help us,' Ofeefee whispered.

'Mama!' Dudu wailed. 'She will be in danger!'

They stared in the direction of the women and saw they had gathered in a crowd and were singing! They were singing the Egba people's song with voices raised against the sounds of war.

'Abeokuta ilu Egba, (Abeokuta, Egba land,)
Ibe l'agbe bi mi si oo. (That's where I was born.)
Emi o f'Abeokuta sogo, (Abeokuta will be my pride,)
Un o duro l'ori Olumo, (I'll stand on the Olumo Rock,)
Emi o maayo l'ori Olumo, (I'll always rejoice on
*   Olumo Rock,)*
Wipe ilu olokiki o, (In a famous town,)
L'awa Egba n gbe e e. (We, the Egba live.)

Un ko nii gbagbe e re, (I'll never forget you,)
Ile ominira. (The land of freedom.)'

The twins looked up at Olumo, standing powerfully above them, and they prayed.

One of the warriors had noticed the women singing and charged towards them. They stood their ground, raising sticks and machetes and singing louder. The hideous, wide-chested and broad-shouldered warrior charged as if mad with anger. An Egba man gave chase, but the warrior swung around mid-stride, plunging his machete into the man's belly.

The women shrieked in fear, but continued singing. The warrior kneeled beside the body of the man and in one swift movement, struck off his head. When the warrior swung the head, dripping with blood, up to the sky, his vest opened and the curve of two heavy breasts were revealed.

'The warriors are women! The warriors are women!' someone screamed.

There were roars of anger from the walls and the slashing continued even more fiercely.

The twins watched the full-chested woman with stunned fascination. Her muscular arms glinted in the hot sun as she brandished the head of the man she had just killed.

She held it up high. 'Yes! We are the Agojie!' she shrieked. 'We are the King's warriors and we are women!

We shall conquer or die!' Her red-and-black-painted face turned fiery when she noticed two Egba men running towards her. She aimed her bow and arrow, but the men were faster and struck her down with brutal slashes of their machetes.

Immediately, a swarm of arrows from the wall hit the men, who fell, screaming.

The Egba women dispersed in all directions, shouting: 'The warriors are women oh!'

Dudu and Ofeefee ducked their heads and ran towards the fighting, Dudu dragging Ofeefee behind her, dodging the screaming women. More people scattered, more arrows fell.

'There!' Dudu pointed. Their mother was among a group of women carrying and stacking sacks and bricks and sticks and anything they could find against the wall.

'Mama!' the twins called at the same time, their voices shrieks of relief. They ran, but their mother waved them away frantically. She snatched up the bottom of her long wrapper and rushed to meet them.

'Back to hiding,' she shouted, her eyes wide with fear. But as she reached them, she stumbled and fell, her eyes bulging. An arrow protruded from her back.

'Mama,' the girls screamed. They caught her and heaved her along, their faces twisted with effort.

Their mother moaned, 'I cannot find air.'

The girls cried out in alarm.

'Take me to the mission,' she coughed.

'The mission?' Dudu asked, glancing at Ofeefee in surprise. 'To the white man?'

'Do you think his god can help you?' Ofeefee asked, eyes brimming with hopeful tears.

'Take me there,' their mother gasped.

'I thought you said he was a stupid storyteller and his god was useless?' Dudu asked.

'But he has medicine,' Ofeefee said.

Their mother tried to speak, but began coughing. She spat blood into her hand.

'Oh, Mama! Please, Mama, don't leave us, stay awake,' they cried as they struggled on. Their mother slumped over them, one arm across each child's shoulder as they pulled forward, leaving the battleground and the war cries behind.

It took almost an hour to get to the mission, struggling past empty mud houses, the abandoned market place and farmsteads. When they passed Olumo, they mumbled a short prayer to the god of the rock. Then, with renewed courage they continued to the other side of the city where the mission was built when the white man came to Abeokuta.

When they approached the large house with its shiny metal roof, the only one of its kind, the whole place looked deserted. There were no busy clergymen

SISTER SPIRIT

preaching or giving advice, no children chanting
words from the white man's holy book. Not a single
person to be seen outside. On the large rock behind
the house they spotted the white man. He was
watching the battleground in the distance. Gunshots
ripped through the air at regular intervals and could
be heard clearly.

'Mama, where should we go now?' Dudu whispered
as they hid behind a tree.

The white man's bald head was shiny and almost as
red as a palm nut. He wiped sweat off his forehead with
a cloth while clutching his holy book tight to his chest
and mumbling nervously into his bushy grey beard. A
young Egba man with blood-stained trousers stumbled
over from the other side of the church. He was hobbling
and panting harshly. The white man scrambled down
and hurried towards him.

The white man's pale wife peered out of the church
and ran to them, followed by another, younger white
man and two Egba converts. They must have been
praying inside the church.

'The Balogun asked me to inform you of what is
happening,' the man with the bloodied trousers called.
He gasped to catch his breath.

'What is the situation? Is there enough ammunition?'
The white man's tongue sounded soft and slippery as he
spoke in Yoruba.

'It is mad women that have attacked the Egba people on this day!' the scout cried.

'What? What do you mean?' the people before him asked.

'Yes, they are women,' he said. 'They broke in through the wall, but we have forced them back.'

'Oh Lord, help us,' the white man's wife said and made a sign across her chest.

'Not here,' the mother wheezed, tightening her grip on the twins' shoulders. 'The house on the other side of the church.' Her words were barely a whisper and she looked pale.

The girls dragged her through the trees behind the church. They stopped as a white man came around the huts, leading a horse. He was younger than the father of the church, with wide shoulders and a trim moustache. A large brimmed hat shaded his face from the sun. The horse was packed with heavy bags out of which jutted a long musket.

He stiffened and looked around hastily, as if to check that no one else could see them.

'What happened?' he hissed as he came closer.

'Mama,' Dudu whispered. 'Who is this man? Do you know him?'

Their mother did not reply. She stared at the man and to the astonishment of the girls, there were tears in her eyes.

'She is hurt,' Ofeefee said, as the man took their mother's weight off their shoulders. He carried her as if she was a bag of leaves and hurried to a nearby hut.

'I have tried my best,' their mother gasped. 'But the people have rejected us. The children will have no one to care for them as I have no family.' She began to choke and struggle for air.

'Shh,' the man said. 'You should not strain yourself. I will attend to your wound and you will be fine.'

The mother shook her head, her face twisted in pain. 'My time has come. Please swear to me, in the name of your white god, that you will take care of them.'

The man dropped her on to her side on the mud bed and stared at her in shock. 'I am a trader,' he said. 'A traveller! Even now I am on my way back to Lagos with a message for the captain and then I will continue to England. I cannot care for them.'

'I have never asked anything of you. Look at them. They are yours as sure as day follows night and night follows day.'

The man turned around to look at the twins.

It was then they saw his bright green eyes, the same shade as their own.

He shook his head and turned back to her. 'I cannot do anything for them. I ... I can give them some money, but that is all.'

'I thought you were a man of your god,' their

mother urged weakly. 'I thought your god was kind. Is that not what you preached to me when you wanted me to leave mine?'

'You do not understand,' he said. 'It is not possible! They are not legitimate. These things are complicated!'

'Swear it!' their mother shrieked with one last breath. She clutched his arm, gripping it in convulsion.

'Mama,' the girls cried. 'God of the Rock, help us, please! Look at your daughter and give her life. Blow life into her body!'

'Stop it,' the man hissed. 'Stop these heathen prayers!'

The girls went rigid at his words. They stared at their mother, lying still and lifeless on the mud bed.

'It is no use,' he said with a frown. 'No one can help her now.'

The man got up. The twins huddled together in a corner, whimpering. He took off his hat and thrust a shaky hand through his hair. A dark patch of sweat had stuck his shirt to his back. His eyes were ablaze as he paced the room cursing quietly. Once in a while he would look at the girls.

Then he drew his breath sharply. He walked up and grabbed Ofeefee by the arm, pulling her away from Dudu and towards the door of the hut.

'I am sorry, child,' he said to Dudu. 'I cannot take you with me.' His voice was strangled. 'Where I am going, there is no place for you.'

'No!' Ofeefee screamed and tried to pull free.

'But why?' Dudu asked. 'Why will you take my half and leave me behind?'

But as she watched him turn away, dragging her screaming sister, she knew the answer. Ofeefee was the colour of his people. Even though they had been born out of the same place, on the same day, connected by one and the same cord. Even though they had fed from the same breasts, her sister was Ofeefee, the pale colour of his people, while she was Dudu, the colour of black, of the Egbas.

'Go to the mission,' the man called, as he mounted the horse behind Ofeefee. 'They take care of orphans, they will take care of you.'

'Please, baba mi, my father,' she called. 'I am your blood too!'

'I am sorry,' he said, avoiding her eyes. Dudu ran beside the horse as it began to gallop away.

'Sisters of one cord and one heart,' she called, stretching her hand towards her. Ofeefee reached out her hand to Dudu, repeating the words.

Then Dudu stumbled and fell. Dust filled her nose, gagging and blinding her. She struggled to her feet and ran as quickly as her little legs could carry her all the way to Olumo, the one place she knew she would be safe. She swore as she ran, mumbling words and magical chants she had heard from her mother.

'Cursed be the day you were born,' she muttered. 'Cursed be your entire lineage.'

When she reached Olumo she placed her small trembling hands on the warm rock. 'Bring me back, my sister, oh God of this Rock. I will do anything, as long as you bring her back to me. I will sacrifice anything you ask.'

She scrambled up fast, her lungs bursting as she reached the top. She scanned the wide horizon, not caring about the bloody scene of battle at her feet. She searched until she saw the thin red, dusty trail of the horse, taking Ofeefee from Abeokuta. The dusty trail that was tearing half of her own self away.

She stretched her hands towards her sister and wailed,

'I ... ke ... ji ... mi!'

47

The pain in my chest was so fierce I thrashed and writhed for several long seconds before I could catch my breath.

The memory of what had happened was as vivid as if I had just been thrown out of the nineteenth century. Gunpowder still burned my nostrils, and my tongue was dry with dust. The thick blanket of darkness enclosing Funmi 14 had me groping around blindly after the bright sunshine.

I came to myself slowly, trying to stop the rush of tears.

For the first time I understood. It wasn't *Jimi*. It was *Ikejimi*, or rather *Ìkeji mi,* which was Yoruba! The agony of its meaning seared through me, tearing me apart so my body felt like it was severed in two.

My other half.

I was breathless. Their own father had separated them, taking one twin to England and leaving the other behind, abandoning Dudu to her fate.

Anger smouldered in my veins like lava.

How could he? How could he be so cruel?

Suddenly, there was a dim glow beneath the window outside. Cat-like eyes gleamed, staring right at me. I leaped out of bed and lunged to the window, pressing my face to the bars. At first I could see nothing. But then, I saw it – a dark, feline shadow, slouching stealthily between the trees. I stretched out my hand, a gasp caught in my throat.

'Everything okay, Tara?' came Bisi's sleepy voice. The shadow melted into the night, slinking away on silent paws.

I felt like screaming at Bisi to leave me alone. I didn't need her! I didn't need anyone.

'Yes,' I hissed.

She turned over and soon I heard her rhythmic breathing.

The ache in my chest was so strong my entire body was on fire. I knew now why I was here. Who I was! I was not crazy and I was not an abiku.

I was here for a reason. I was only half of myself and I needed to finally become whole.

I cocked my head to the window, listening. There it was! The call was faint, but I could clearly discern the words *Ìkejì mi* over and over.

'Mo n'bọ! I am coming!' I mouthed, stretching out my hand. The Yoruba words felt smooth and natural on my tongue. The wind carried soft sighs of relief towards me and I felt peace.

I took sure, steady steps, feeling my way around prickly bushes, rough trunks and along the cold metal of the fence. I had my torch with me, but I couldn't switch it on while I was out in the open. I was not worried and pushed onward. The shrill chirp of crickets was a sharp, regular beat that drowned out the howling winds. My throat was dry by now from breathing the dust.

The stone felt cool beneath my palms as I slipped through the gap between the fence and the rock.

Slowly, with my back pressed to the rock, I balanced along the edge of the river. The tangy smell of water grass and fish spiced the night air. The ledge was so thin I could only inch forward. The river rippled silvery grey in the darkness below.

I thought of Omi and immediately felt faint, leaning into the rock. My hands were clammy and sweat trickled down the back of my neck. Like me, she'd been plagued by nightmares and a deep longing. Omi had probably been Dudu's descendant and I was most likely of Ofeefee's lineage. We had both felt the pain of their separation. But now I would never meet her. She was dead and I had come too late.

She'd felt drawn to this place too. Was it just coincidence that she died here?

An owl hooted from the other side of the river. Its gloomy call made me nervous. I urged myself onwards, feeling my way along the rock until my fingers found the cave entrance. With a quick movement, I swung myself around and into the cave. I stumbled inside, the torch falling out of my pocket and crashing to the ground. My skin prickled with the sensation of not being alone. I groped around in panic, nails scratching stone, and I gasped when they finally touched the plastic cylinder. With trembling hands, I shone its light into the cave.

There was no one. Only a low, terrifying tunnel curving away into the unknown. I knew this tunnel from my dream.

The energy that had driven me out of Funmi 14 and up to this cave was evaporating. Claustrophobia lay its cold hands around my throat. I took a step back, when I remembered the river behind me. Just in time, I grabbed the rock, steadying myself. A rush of rubble dropped into the river like a warning.

A distant rumbling came out of the cave, gathering in force as its whispers strengthened into a full-blown wail. The sound vibrated through the ground and into the soles of my feet, like an earthquake, penetrating my entire body. I stretched out my arms as the familiar yearning flowed through me. I lunged forward, only stopping to shine the torch to see the way.

The tunnel was irregular, changing from tight cracks to wide caverns and tall archways, then shrinking back to confined cavities. I stumbled on, and visions began to form and race through my head: Ofeefee on the cliffs in England, Dudu on Olumo Rock. I saw Dudu growing up, secluded, always in hiding, living underground in tunnels and caves. Tracing the same path she had walked hundreds of times, I realised I already knew where this tunnel would lead. Eventually it widened, opening into an almost cathedral-like chamber with a pointed ceiling. I was beneath, or rather inside of, Olumo Rock.

I no longer needed my torch because dim light seeped in through a large crack in the roof. It had to be dawn already. I stared up at the mangled disarray of roots creeping across like intertwined snakes.

A whisper shivered through the air beside me and I jumped.

She was here.

48

'Ofeefee, finally you have come,' she said with a voice like feathers.

She was old, extremely old. And beautiful. Her hair was the purest white, falling down her back in long, soft coils. Her skin was so dark in contrast that her deep green eyes glowed with the gravest intensity. Despite her age, I could still see little Dudu, the girl who had been abandoned on that day in 1851 when King Gezo's Amazons attacked.

She came towards me, gliding over the rocky ground. I felt a cold waft of wind and her hand on my cheek.

'My other half,' she said, her voice cracking. 'I knew you would come to me.'

I shuddered, feeling a strange heaviness.

She took my hands in hers and I knew the right words. We spoke them at the same time.

'Sisters of one cord and one heart.'

My words blended into her words, my voice melted into her voice. Our two selves entwined. Time became meaningless as we gazed into each other's eyes.

I saw the now and before. Her love and her loss. A loss too painful to bear. She had rejected it, choosing instead a life of infinite waiting and hope. Her powers had grown out of her love and hate, tethering her to this world ever since. Waiting. Again and again she had reached out to Ofeefee across the ocean, had kept their connection alive. Even beyond Ofeefee's passing, she'd continued the connection between herself, her descendants and Ofeefee's.

She'd reached out to me in England. It was *her* agony I'd felt when Omotara died. I'd felt it in my chest for weeks. *She* had brought me to Nigeria and spoken to me at Olumo Rock to prepare me for what lay ahead.

And I was ready.

She smiled gently, her eyes full of love. When she turned away I could hardly stand it.

'Stay,' I called desperately.

'We must take the last step on our path so we can be together for ever.' She beckoned me and walked to the other end of the cave. I saw that footholds had been carved into the wall, forming steps that led to the roof. She climbed on to the first step, holding out her hand to me and I followed without hesitation. She disappeared through a crack, towards the light which was now fully bright. I was about to heave myself through when I heard a cry.

'Tara! What are you doing?'

I stared in disbelief, annoyed at the interruption.

Bisi and Lanre were shining a torch at me.

'I have to join her. Finally, we will be united,' I said.

'What do you mean?' Lanre called.

'We will be one, and nothing will separate us again,' I said with a relieved smile.

'Tara, you are scaring me,' Bisi called. 'Please come down from there!'

But I squeezed through the tight split in the rock. Daylight blinded me.

She was there, waiting. We were on a protruding ledge halfway up Olumo. The awakening city lay at our feet and behind us soared the smooth, grey face of the rock. Even though I was on a thin ledge, probably more than fifty metres above ground, I wasn't afraid. I felt elated, full of power. A sharp morning breeze rustled my PU as I inched nearer to Dudu, eager to close the distance between us.

A gasp came from behind.

'Tara, oh my god, Tara! You are going to get yourself killed!' I glanced back to see Bisi, her eyes wide in terror as she looked down at the tiny houses below. Lanre gripped her hand and pulled her to a safer spot.

'Tara,' he called. 'Please come back.'

I turned away from them, shuffling until I was beside Dudu.

'Whatever it is you are seeing, Tara, it is just a ghost,' Bisi called. 'We cannot see her!'

'My twin sister is here with me,' I replied. 'I now know the truth. She waited over one hundred and fifty years for me. Finally, we will be united.'

Bisi shook her head. 'Don't allow her pains and memories to take over! They are not your memories. They are not your pains, Tara. Only hers.'

I shut out her voice.

Dudu slipped her hand in mine. 'Ìkejì mi,' she said, and the words were a balm for my aching heart.

'Sisters of one cord and one heart,' we both chanted.

From the corner of my eye, I saw a figure – Lanre. I growled. I wanted Dudu all to myself, like she wanted me for herself. We had been separated for so long. Now we wanted to be together. 'Go back,' I called. 'I don't need you. Stay away!'

But he continued to approach slowly – tiny step after tiny step, his limbs trembling.

'Bisi, please make Lanre go back.'

'She is right,' Bisi called. 'Lanre, it is too dangerous. You are bigger than her. It is too tight for you on the ledge.' Bisi was crying now.

Dudu tugged my hand gently. 'It is time,' she said and my body filled with a warm sensation. I knew what I had to do. I pushed my feet to the edge. I could feel Dudu's spirit enter mine, becoming one with me. She filled the space that had felt so bruised and empty, leaving me confused all my life. It was indescribably beautiful. Every question in me was answered, every doubt appeased, every pain eased. Every crease in my soul was smoothed.

'You are special,' she said. 'Ofeefee couldn't come back. And the others after her ... they didn't know how to find their way. Parallel twins born on opposite sides of the world for generations, but never able to unite. Then Omotara ... ah, she went too early. It was not her time. She and you were supposed to find each other.'

She sighed deeply and I felt the loss of Omotara ripple through me.

'Only you were left. That is why you and I must now unite. You didn't disappoint me. In the end ... you alone knew in which direction to look. You alone understood the messages I sent for you.'

I gasped as I felt her pain. The hurt of Ofeefee being taken away in a trail of dust.

I saw Ofeefee on the cliffs in England and my other sisters that had come after. All of them hurting, broken, until they ended their lives. I saw Ruth, my mother, writing in her blue diary, tears dripping into the ink. I saw myself in the cot behind her. Two-year-old me stretching out my arms to her, snot dripping down my face as I cried. But she did not pick me up. She poured a handful of pills into her trembling hand. Then began to swallow them, one by one.

I sank to my knees, swaying at the pain that overcame me.

The bottle lay on the table, pills scattered around the blue diary. Ruth was sitting at the foot of the cot, holding my hand.

'I love you,' she said. 'Please forgive me!'

'Tara!' It was Lanre's voice again, tearing me from my thoughts.

A wind rushed past, raising dust. Dudu was on my other side, a whirlwind, trying to shield me from Bisi, Lanre and their calls. But I could still see.

'Tara, don't!' he cried, breaking into a fit of coughing as the dust engulfed him and he lost his hold. Bisi's scream ripped through the air as he slipped and fell, melting into the hum of Dudu's calming words.

'The pain will soon be over,' she said. 'Just walk that last step with me. One … last … step.'

49

I placed my hands on the rock to push myself off when Bisi's desperate voice cut through.

'Tara, please! Think of your parents. They love you. They'll be heartbroken.'

I paused. They did love me. Ruth had also loved me. She'd told me.

It was a good feeling to be loved.

The hurt, that my biological mother had given me away, dissolved.

She had loved me. She hadn't wanted to die. None of them had wanted to die.

The warm feeling in my chest ebbed away with this realisation and a searing hot thing took its place. It was anger. My hands curled into fists and my breathing became ragged.

All those lives. Lost!

I saw little Dudu placing her trembling hand on the

rock and swearing, *Bring me back, my sister, oh God of this Rock. I will sacrifice anything!*

For over one and a half centuries, Dudu had sacrificed the lives of so many people, her own family and blood. All because she had refused to accept the loss of Ofeefee.

'No!' I cried, tearing myself out of her grasp.

'Ofeefee!' she screamed. The thread holding me together, the exhilarating wholeness I had just felt, ripped apart, and I gasped at the overwhelming emptiness surging through me. But for the first time since meeting her, I could think clearly.

'I am not Ofeefee,' I said. 'Ofeefee is dead! Your curse killed her.'

Dudu shook her head, covering her face with old, arthritic hands.

'You killed Ofeefee because you didn't release her. She died a terrible death, lonely and heartbroken. You never allowed her to lead a happy life, to find peace.'

'No,' Dudu cried, shaking her head. 'Ofeefee has come back to me!'

'Ofeefee is dead. You killed her and her daughter and her granddaughter and her great-granddaughter and—'

'Noooo!' Dudu screamed.

I shuddered, tears seeping from my eyes. I could hardly bear her pain because her pain was still mine. But she had to understand. I thought of poor Omi and her nightmares.

'You ruined the lives of those in your own lineage. Your great-great-great-granddaughter Omotara suffered nightmares and died like those before her, because, like me, she was drawn to your call, never understanding what was missing in her life.'

Dudu tried to take my hands in hers, but I pulled away, pressing my back firmly into the rock.

'No,' I cried. 'You can't have my life as well. Can't you see that this horrible vendetta has to end?'

Dudu's green eyes were beginning to blur. Her face, her hair, everything was fading.

She screamed, her face contorting with fear. She stretched her arms towards me and I reached out to her, feeling my heart break.

'Ìkejì mi!' she cried and her silhouette curled up – her green eyes, sharp canines and skin, all fading. One last cry and she fell off the rock and was gone.

'My sister spirit,' I whispered, sobbing, for the pain of one hundred and fifty years.

Frantic grunts and scrambling sounds brought me back. Lanre was hanging from the ledge, his chin pressed to a sharp rock that jutted out and sweat rolled down his face. Bisi was making her way towards the ledge where he'd slipped and lost his balance and she was shaking so hard it looked like she too might fall. I edged towards him from the other side, terror hitting me full force.

'Hold on, Lanre,' I whispered.

'You don't need to tell me that,' he hissed through clenched teeth. 'That's the only thought on my mind right now.'

His arms had begun to tremble as well.

Bisi and I kneeled on either side of him and grabbed one arm each.

I glanced at her. We would have to hold his entire weight. She nodded and at the same time we pulled, loosening his grip from the ledge. He roared in fear. His life was in our hands.

With muscles that felt like they were tearing and with more strength than I thought we had, Bisi and I heaved him up beside us. I let out a cry of relief, breaking into tears as we clutched each other tightly.

50

'Lola was in a very bad state when we left,' Bisi said, breaking the silence as we stumbled back through the tunnels.

'Why?' I asked, shooting a quick glance at Lanre. He still looked stunned. My voice was thin and hoarse and I was grateful for anything that would take my mind off all that had happened.

'Lola was the one who discovered you were missing.'

'Oh.' I hadn't even considered how Bisi and Lanre had found me.

'She searched the entire dorm and then had a nervous breakdown and woke us. She kept shouting: "Tara is gone, just like Omi." She said it was her fault because she'd told you things about Omi. That you would die too.'

'Mrs Abimbola shushed Lola up and dragged her into her office. She was acting really weird. She said Lola was having psychological issues and she actually locked her up!'

'What?' I cried.

'I'm telling you! It was scary! The whole dorm had woken by then, many of the girls were crying. We heard Lola screaming and breaking things in Mrs Abimbola's office.'

I walked faster, feeling awful about the chaos I'd caused. Lola had gone through so much already.

'Mrs Abimbola sent everyone back to bed. As if anyone could sleep after that! She gathered all the prefects from the girls' and boys' dorms to go searching for you. I snuck to the office door and told Lola not to worry, that we were going to find you. Lola said she was sure you went to the cave where the wailing came from. She said that was where Omi died and that it had something to do with the nightmares you both had. That you were somehow connected. I snuck out, got hold of Lanre who was searching the grounds with the other prefects, and we came looking for you.'

'I don't know what would have happened if you hadn't,' I whispered and felt Lanre's hand reach for mine.

'What a night!' Bisi said. 'I had never even heard of this girl, Omi, before today.'

'Omi was my parallel twin. Her name was Omotara and she had my bunk before me. I had a feeling we were somehow connected. Then I found her sketchbook and knew for sure. She was Lola's close friend.'

'Wow – she had your name and your bunk just a year before you came? What a coincidence!'

'No, it was part of the curse bringing us back to this place. To Dudu.' My heart thudded painfully at her name.

'I will never again say I do not believe in juju or ghost stories,' Bisi whispered. 'At first we didn't see her. We thought you'd gone mad. It looked like you were talking to yourself. But out on the ledge, when she seemed to become part of you, we saw her entering and then leaving you. It was terrifying, Tara! Those piercing green eyes!' Bisi shuddered and the trail of light from her torch shuddered too.

'She was my great-great-great-grandmother's twin sister. But she's gone now. For good.' I took a deep breath. 'I'll tell you the full story some other time.'

'Are you all right?' I asked, turning to Lanre, who still hadn't uttered a word.

'Yes, all good. I'm okay. Just a bit ... blown away.'

'What I don't understand is how I never heard that this girl Omi died?' Bisi said. 'I can't believe someone in our room died on school grounds, and no one ever mentioned it.'

'Lola and Mrs Abimbola were the only ones who knew.'

Lola had spilled the secret despite Mrs Abimbola's threats. I felt sick. She could get expelled, or worse, if it all came out now.

'Did you know her, Lanre?' Bisi asked.

'To be honest, I hadn't heard of her until recently,' Lanre said. 'I asked Theo why Lola was being so mean to you, Tara, and if he couldn't talk her into leaving you alone, him being her cousin and all. Sorry … for not minding my business…'

'Hey, I'm touched by your concern,' I said, and smiled.

'He told me Lola had lost her best friend, hinting something terrible had happened. He said how badly it had affected and changed Lola. I felt sorry for her. But I didn't realise her friend had actually died in school.'

'Lola told me Mrs Abimbola covered everything up, even getting rid of the body, and threatened her.'

'Oh my god!' Lanre and Bisi cried together.

'Lola had kept quiet all this while, but now … I hope she won't get into trouble. I feel responsible.'

Finally, the tunnel brightened and soon we heard the river outside.

'Oh, thank goodness,' Bisi cried, rushing forward.

As we helped each other cross the last ledge, there was the sound of voices and a commotion in front of the little rock.

'This is all rubbish!' Mrs Abimbola cried angrily. 'No one ever died here! The students were scared when

EFUA TRAORÉ

they couldn't find Tara, and you know how girls are, they panicked and started rumours. This useless man should be fired for spreading such a horrific story. Get rid of him!'

I made a sign to Bisi and Lanre to be quiet. We peeked around the rock. The principal and Mrs Abimbola were arguing and beside them the gardener was being held down by two guards. He was trembling and dishevelled, like there had been a fight.

Mrs Abimbola saw us and pointed frantically. 'There she is! You see! These students have found her! Did I not say nobody goes missing on my watch? Away with him!'

'Not so quickly,' the principal interrupted. He gestured to one of the guards to help us over the fence.

'I know wetin I see that night! My mind never rest since that day. I know wetin I see!' the gardener cried. 'And I know the student wey find the girl. Na one slim girl. She also knows. She be witness!'

'Goodness, someone shut this illiterate up, for heaven's sake!'

'Mrs Abimbola, please, can we remain respectful here? I'm sure we can solve the problem without raising our voices,' our principal said. He didn't look as neatly dressed as usual, his blue shirt was rumpled and partly untucked, but his voice was calm.

'Will you please let go of Mr Akpan?' he said to the guards. 'He is a witness, for goodness' sake, not under

294

arrest!' He turned to us and nodded. 'Everything okay? No one hurt?'

'No one hurt, Sir,' Lanre said.

'Everything fine, Sir!' Bisi called.

'Okay, good, you had us very worried.' He turned to me. 'You have some serious questions to answer later.'

I swallowed, wondering what my explanation would be.

'Who is this other student, this witness?' he asked the gardener.

'I no know her name, but I go fit recognise am.'

'Her name is Lola. In Funmi 14.' I said, ignoring Mrs Abimbola's menacing look.

'Rubbish!' Mrs Abimbola cried. 'I have called the psychiatric clinic to come for her. Lola has serious problems. We've had a lot of issues recently. She even cut off another girl's hair!'

'You called the psychiatric clinic without informing me? Have her parents been informed?' The principal was visibly angry now.

'Mrs Abimbola locked Lola in her office at five a.m. She is probably still in there now,' Bisi jumped in.

'You did what? Okay, this has gone too far. We are talking about allegations of an unreported death. A death being covered up.'

He pulled a phone out of his trouser pocket. 'I'm calling the police.'

51

After months of wearing our PUs, it was weird seeing Bisi in an oversized white T-shirt knotted over baggy jeans and a chain belt. I looked down at my own slim fit, ripped jeans and felt odd.

The different colours in the hall were almost painful after months of uniform grey. A stylish woman in a skirt-suit in bright Ankara material and high heels caught my eye. She was talking into airpods and gesturing dramatically. To my surprise, Bisi waved and went over to hug her. So that was her mum!

'This is my friend, Tara,' Bisi said, smiling as I approached.

'Thank you for driving me back to Lagos and letting me stay over until my flight tomorrow night.'

'It's no problem, Tara,' the woman said with a quick smile. 'I am so happy Bisi has found a good friend here. Because of you, she has finally settled in.' While she was speaking, she was scoping the room. 'Where is Lanre? We need to be off.'

'He should be here any moment,' Bisi said.

Her mum nodded. 'Okay, I'll go and sign the three of you out. Have your bags ready. Okay, Gladys, I'm here, when did you say the delivery will be?' She was back to her conversation on the phone and hurried away.

Bisi rolled her eyes. 'That's my mum for you,' she said.

I grinned.

'Hey, Bisi!' A girl I recognised from another dorm was waving. Bisi walked up to chat with her and I looked around the hall, my belly jumping. I was going to Lagos with Bisi and Lanre. Being with them outside of the dorm and school would be fun. We were dropping Lanre off but planned to meet at the beach the next day before my flight back home.

'Hey!' Lanre said, showing up beside me. He was wearing a dark-blue T-shirt and jeans and looked extremely hot. When I glanced at his face, he avoided my eyes. He'd been acting this way all week.

'Happy to be going home?' he asked awkwardly.

'Yes! I've missed my parents.'

An uncomfortable silence stretched between us.

Bisi came back giggling, and when she saw us, placed her hands on her hips.

'Okay, this has gone on too long!' she said to Lanre

and turned to face me. 'Lanre thinks you're not coming back in January.'

Lanre rolled his eyes. 'Amebo! Why can't you go about your own business, Bisi?'

'Because I can't stand seeing you guys like this after all we've been through.' Her voice was low and serious. 'We don't need secrets,' she continued. 'I mean, come on, we are friends, aren't we?'

I stared at Lanre, confused. 'Why would you think that?'

He shrugged and avoided looking at me. 'Well, you found what you were looking for, didn't you? Your roots. Your story. Okay, you didn't find your biological dad, but he is probably in Europe anyway, where he met your mum. You'd have better chances finding him there. So, you have nothing keeping you here. Do you?'

With those last words he met my eyes and looked so pained my heart skipped a beat.

'Hey,' I said, taking his hand in mine and squeezing it. 'This trip has been ... mind-blowing, world-changing...'

Lanre looked disappointed. 'I know,' he said.

'But not the way you might think,' I added. 'Yes, I finally know my story and I can breathe freely for the first time in my life. But I didn't only find my roots, I found a second home. You and Bisi are what makes Nigeria home to me.'

'Aaaww!' Bisi smiled.

'I don't even want to continue searching for my biological dad. At least not right now. It wasn't him I was looking for on this journey anyway. I was looking for myself.'

I glanced at them, feeling shy, but they gave me encouraging nods.

'I don't have many friends back home. To be honest, I had exactly one and I didn't treat her very nicely so I have to fix that.' I had hopes, though, because I'd been texting Maxine recently, and we'd made plans to meet over the holidays. I had a lot of explaining to do, but she replied that she'd be happy to see me.

'I could never open up to others,' I continued, 'because I never understood myself. Things are different now. I'm excited about going home – for the first time I might actually feel at ease.'

Lanre looked more desolate by the second.

'But I would not miss coming back for all the world.' My eyes filled with tears at the realisation. 'Nothing will stop me finishing my year at Olumo Haven with you guys.'

Lanre grinned sheepishly. 'Okay, okay, then,' he said, raising his hands. 'If you'd told me how pathetic your life in England was, then of course I would have believed you right away.'

I punched him in the arm.

'Ouch,' he cried, laughing.

'Don't get me wrong, I can't wait for two weeks of privacy in my own room.'

Bisi grinned. 'I feel you, my sista,' she said and we knocked our fists together laughing.

Someone waved at me. It was Lola. 'January,' she yelled across the hall.

'January,' I called back with a smile. I would never have thought it possible, but Lola and I got on well now. She'd changed drastically. Since the weight of keeping Omi's death a secret was taken away, the bitterness and meanness had left her.

After our new dorm mistress arrived, things calmed down. Lola had not been punished. The principal felt sympathy for her losing her friend and having to keep silent about her death. Her relationship with Omi was never analysed in detail. Mrs Abimbola packed her things and we'd heard there was a court case.

They never found Omi's body. But there was a farewell ceremony. A memorial had been set up near the little rock behind the school. A stone that read: *Gone, but not forgotten.*

Only two people, Lola and I, cared that she was gone. And I hadn't even known her.

Bisi's mum appeared in the doorway of the reception hall and beckoned us to come.

We grabbed our bags and rushed outside to the car park.

In the distance, the outline of Olumo Rock stood majestically.

I nodded, holding my head high and feeling strangely proud. Finally I knew who I was and where I came from.

Like the Egba people centuries ago, I too had reached the end of my wanderings.

About the Author

Efua Traoré is a Nigerian-German author of three children's books which have been translated into numerous languages. She has won the *Times/ ChickenHouse* prize, the Commonwealth short story prize and the Zilveren Griffel award. Her debut novel was shortlisted for the Waterstones Children's book prize and was awarded the *Times* children's book of the year. *Sister Spirit* is her first novel for older readers.

Acknowledgements

I owe a load of gratitude to my agent Clare Wallace. Thank you for believing in *Sister Spirit*, for your brilliant insight and for making me do those rewrites, even though I sighed each time.

A huge thank you to Lauren Atherton, for being so enthusiastic and welcoming and to all the other brilliant people in the Zephyr team.

I am forever grateful to my family for their unwavering love and support. Time and again you have shown me that I am never alone, thank you. Shola, Enina and Leila, you make me happier and prouder than you can ever know. I want to be a better, stronger person for you.

Heartfelt thanks to Blain, my lovely sis for sharing her experiences with me. Listening to you is always inspiring.

Thank you Camilla Ru @thecamru for this gorgeous cover I love so much. It's more beautiful than I could have imagined.

Also to my brilliant Yoruba teacher, Boluwatife Ogunlade, for your help whenever I have Yoruba questions and for your patience in teaching me all those ton-marks.

And to Richard Pickard and Faridah Abike-Iyimide for listening and for your encouragements.

Finally, as always, thank you to all my readers.

Author's note

The setting of *Sister Spirit* was inspired by a visit I made to Olumo Rock in Nigeria. I was fascinated by the ancient rock and its priestess, Iya Orisha Olumo (mother goddess of Olumo), who lived there until 2002 at the age of 136, witnessing the coronation of four kings.

Olumo Rock protected the Yoruba for centuries, witnessing inter-tribal wars, invasions by the Dahomian female warriors, missionaries and colonialists. Sitting high on one of its boulders, I sensed its magical presence, as if the rock wanted to tell me the things it had seen. Little did I know then that I would draw on this moment years later for my story.

I love how juju and superstitions still drift around modern life in Nigeria like whispery spirits that refuse to move on. The air bristles with the possibility of the supernatural. Spine-chilling tales about night creatures, haunted rivers, vengeful lady koi koi visiting boarding schools or evil spirits like the abiku, trigger my imagination and have me looking for a sheet of paper.

Writing this story about Tara's journey in search of her roots and, ultimately, herself, felt close to my heart. That feeling of not truly belonging, of not fully understanding yourself, is one I have often struggled with. I hope I have written Tara's perspective with due respect and sensitivity. I have had enlightening discussions with adopted people and adoptive parents, but I do not want to claim I know what it means to grow up adopted (especially transracially). Instead, I wrote from a perspective I know well: of feeling different, and sometimes disconnected, from those around you.

Growing up in Nigeria as a child of Nigerian-German heritage, then moving to Europe, had me musing over identity and the meaning of home. Being brown in a world of mostly black or mostly white people, not looking like your parents, means you are constantly asked — where do you come from? Where is home? As if you don't belong...

I also felt close to Lola, hurting along with her, as she struggled to find her place. Homosexuality is criminalised by law in Nigeria. Queer people are persecuted and arrested simply for being who they are. I believe that every human being should have the right to be themselves and to love who they want to.

Love is a beautiful, powerful thing. The idea for this book came through a vision of two sisters, separated. Two hearts torn apart. Anyone who has ever truly loved should understand.

At the end, Tara finds her answer. Nigeria calms her restless spirit and she can return to her parents. While writing this story, I came to realise that home is not a physical place. Home is finding peace within yourself, feeling loved. Home is a place in your heart.

Efua Traoré
Munich
2024

Zephyr is an imprint of Head of Zeus.
At Zephyr we are proud to publish books
you can read and re-read time and time
again because they tell a brilliant story
and because they entertain you.

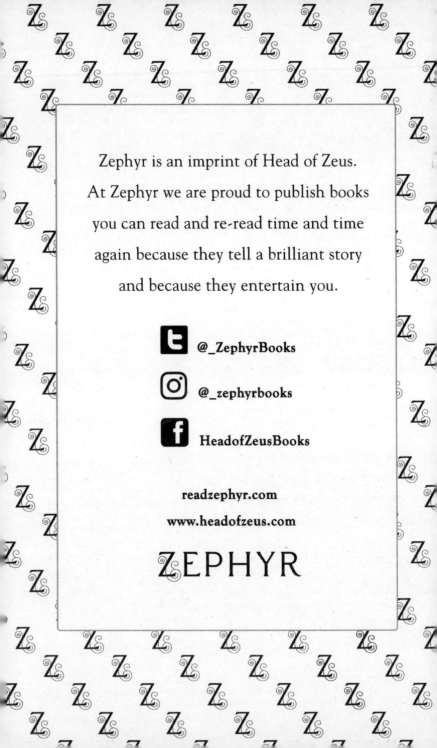 @_ZephyrBooks

@_zephyrbooks

HeadofZeusBooks

readzephyr.com

www.headofzeus.com

ZEPHYR